Strength & Power

The Chronicles of Kerrigan, Volume 10

W.J. May

Published by Dark Shadow Publishing, 2016.

This is a work of fiction. Similarities to real people, places, or events are entirely coincidental.

STRENGTH & POWER

First edition. April 15, 2016.

Copyright © 2016 W.J. May.

Also by W.J. May

Bit-Lit Series
Lost Vampire
Cost of Blood
Price of Death

Blood Red Series
Courage Runs Red
The Night Watch
Marked by Courage
Forever Night

Daughters of Darkness: Victoria's Journey
Huntress
Coveted (A Vampire & Paranormal Romance)
Victoria

Hidden Secrets Saga
Seventh Mark - Part 1
Seventh Mark - Part 2
Marked By Destiny
Compelled
Fate's Intervention
Chosen Three

The Chronicles of Kerrigan
Rae of Hope
Dark Nebula
House of Cards
Royal Tea
Under Fire

End in Sight
Hidden Darkness
Twisted Together
Mark of Fate
Strength & Power

The Chronicles of Kerrigan Prequel
Christmas Before the Magic

The Hidden Secrets Saga
Seventh Mark (part 1 & 2)

The Senseless Series
Radium Halos
Radium Halos - Part 2
Nonsense

The X Files
Code X
Replica X

Standalone
Shadow of Doubt (Part 1 & 2)
Five Shades of Fantasy
Glow - A Young Adult Fantasy Sampler
Shadow of Doubt - Part 2
Four and a Half Shades of Fantasy
Full Moon
Dream Fighter
What Creeps in the Night
Forest of the Forbidden
HuNted
Arcane Forest: A Fantasy Anthology
Ancient Blood of the Vampire and Werewolf

The Chronicles of Kerrigan

Strength & Power

Book X

By

W.J. May

Copyright 2016 by W.J. May

The Chronicles of Kerrigan

Book I - *Rae of Hope* is FREE!
  Book Trailer:
  http://www.youtube.com/watch?v=gILAwXxx8MU
  Book II - *Dark Nebula*
  Book Trailer:
  http://www.youtube.com/watch?v=Ca24STi_bFM
  Book III - *House of Cards*
  Book IV - *Royal Tea*
  Book V - *Under Fire*
  Book VI - *End in Sight*
  Book VII – *Hidden Darkness*
  Book VIII – *Twisted Together*
  Book IX – *Mark of Fate*
  Book X – *Strength & Power*
  Book XI – *Last One Standing*
  Coming May 2016
  Book XII – *Rae of Light*
  Coming June 2016
  PREQUEL – Christmas Before the Magic

Chronicles of Kerrigan Prequel

A Novella of the Chronicles of Kerrigan.
A prequel on how Simon Kerrigan met Beth!!
AVAILABLE NOW

Find W.J. May

Website:
http://www.wanitamay.yolasite.com
Facebook:
https://www.facebook.com/pages/Author-WJ-May-FAN-
PAGE/141170442608149
Newsletter:
SIGN UP FOR W.J. May's Newsletter to find out about new
releases, updates, cover reveals and even freebies!
http://eepurl.com/97aYf

Description:

Strength & Power is the 10th Book of W.J. May's bestselling series, The Chronicles of Kerrigan.

"Life doesn't always make sense, and the heart doesn't always understand what the head realizes."

Rae Kerrigan has proven herself a vital asset to the Privy Council and yet, they still question her loyalty.

So Rae and Devon are broken up. Gabriel's furious he wasn't chosen. Angel is back in the picture, Kraigan is out of the picture, and Molly and Luke have turned into one of those hilarious obnoxious perfect couples...

After discovering a cryptic clue left by her father, Rae Kerrigan finds herself facing off against an opponent she never expected: the Privy Council. The lines between 'good' and 'evil' are blurred once again, only this time, Rae isn't sure who's left on her side. Life in London becomes a dangerous dance—one she must navigate carefully because the stakes have never been higher.

Could it be possible the Council was behind everything all along? Is Rae really willing to cut all ties and go rogue like her father? How far will the agents at Guilder go to stop her?

Who might she be leaving behind...?

Strength & Power is the 10th book in the Chronicles of Kerrigan series.

Book 1, Rae of Hope is currently FREE.

Follow Rae Kerrigan as she learns about the tattoo on her back that gives her supernatural powers, as she learns of her father's evil intentions and as she tries to figure out how coming of age, falling love and high-packed action fighting isn't as easy as the comic books make it look.

Series Order:
Rae of Hope
Dark Nebula
House of Cards
Royal Tea
Under Fire
End in Sight
Hidden Darkness
Twisted Together
Mark of Fate
Strength & Power
Last One Standing
Rae of Light
Prequel: Christmas Before the Magic

Chapter 1

'It was the best of times; it was the worst of times...'
Charles Dickens

Yeah, well, it was mostly just the worst of times. But who was I to complain?

Rae Kerrigan sat in the backseat of a taxi, watching the city blur by. After an impromptu visit to Scotland, followed by an even more impromptu visit to the northern coast, she was finally back home where she belonged.

Well, she was back in London. Home might be stretching it a bit.

"Another time around the square, Miss?"

She leaned her head against the window with a quiet sigh, then circled her fingers in the air. "I'm afraid so, Billy. Just keep them coming."

With an obliging smile, he flipped on the turn signal and steered them back around the way they'd just come.

Thanks to the help of her new friend, Billy-the-cab-driver, Rae had circled her apartment no fewer than seven times. Any other day, she'd have been excited to go in. To share the news of what she'd found in her mother's barn and at Dunnett Head. To pore over every word of the letter her father had left her. To ride triumphantly into PC headquarters and present them with the final piece of Simon Kerrigan's brainwashing device.

Yes, any other day, she'd have been excited to go in.

But today...she didn't quite know what was waiting there for her.

As the cab circled once more around the residential square, she stared through the steamy glass, her heart pounding like a butterfly on speed. On one side of the street towered her penthouse, the same penthouse where she'd recently kissed a man who wasn't her boyfriend. On the other side stretched a park she had once found lovely, the same park where said boyfriend had, hours later, broken up with her.

Broken up...*for* her, she mentally reminded herself. But the longer she thought about it, deep down, she wasn't sure if that was true.

No matter what Devon said to deny it, no matter how many ways he phrased it so that their time apart was for her benefit—it had to be for his benefit as well. At least a little. She had kissed Gabriel. Not by accident, not on a whim. Because a part of her wanted to know what it was like.

There was no way Devon was just alright with that. There was no way he didn't need space.

And while Rae had never been more sure of their relationship, never been more certain that Devon Wardell was the only future she would ever desire—charging back in with guns blazing to get him back was probably not the best move right now.

She'd messed up. She'd gone and hurt him. Worst of all, she'd made him doubt her feelings for him. No. She wasn't going to march in and make a speech to get him back. She was going to do him the exact same courtesy he had done for her.

She was going to give him time.

And while he was taking time, she had a few things to work out on her own.

For the millionth time that day, her fingers drifted down into her pocket, lightly tracing the two things they found there. The first was something she'd almost been expecting—the missing piece of the puzzle. The final palladium shard that completed her father's brainwashing device. It was small, only about the size of a quarter, and oddly striking. Its iridescent color and jagged yet symmetrical shape was nothing like the other pieces they had recovered. The very essence of it had seemed to almost glow as she'd extracted it from the ground beneath the maple.

Truth be told, she'd almost stopped digging the second she found it, thinking her mission complete. What else could her father possibly have left to hide? Fortunately, in the glowing Scottish sunset another glint of light had caught her eye, and she had proceeded to dig a little further.

As if mimicking her thoughts, her fingers travelled slowly to the other item nestled safely in her jacket pocket. It was even smaller than the first, and smooth like granite or marble. Rae didn't know what kind of stone it was, nor did she know what the carved inscription on it meant. It wasn't in any language she understood. The only thing she recognized was her father's handwriting.

Vetitum

With a sigh of frustration, she pulled it out into the open and held it up to the light for a closer examination.

Why so many clues? Why the cryptic letters from the grave? Why did all of her searches for the truth seem to lead her to places like cemeteries and secret tombs?

Couldn't anybody ever just say exactly what they meant? Was that too much to ask for? A little bit of well-deserved clarity?

Why not just come out and say: 'Hey, Rae. It's Dad. Sorry for all the killing. On a side note, I no longer trust the Privy Council because of A, B, and C. Good luck with everything!'

Rae rolled her eyes. Why? Because then he wouldn't be a criminal mastermind, and she wouldn't be the daughter eternally cursed with picking up the pieces. That's why.

"What'cha got there?" Billy called, eying her through the partition. "Jewelry?"

She glanced up in surprise, realizing she was still holding up the stone for all the world to see. "No, it's a...it's my lucky rock."

Great excuse, super spy. That's why they pay you the big bucks.

"That's...interesting," he said politely, trying to allow her to save face. "So what do you say?" He gestured out the window and she followed his gaze to see that they were, once more, parked in front of the apartment. "Want to try to get out this time?"

Come on, Kerrigan. Show a little backbone.

She nodded hastily and reached for the door. But the second her fingers touched the handle, an image of Devon's heartbroken, devastated face flashed through her mind. She jerked back like she'd touched fire, and shot Billy an apologetic look through the partition.

"Just...once more around the block?"

He chuckled and eased them back into traffic. "Whatever you want, honey. It's your money. I just watch the meter. And the road."

"Right."

As they circled around for what she hoped was the last time, she gathered her purse up into her lap and tried to come up with a game plan.

I'll just go inside, say I'm sorry to anyone else who needs to hear, and tell everyone what happened in Scotland. They'll help me decode the stone, I'll deliver the final piece to the Privy Council, Devon will realize I'm as certain about us as he is, and everything...everything will just go back to normal.

Yes. High fives all around. That sounded like a good plan.

...Right?

But the longer she turned it over in her mind, the more and more unsettled she became.

Everything would just go back to normal? They were a little bit past that now, weren't they?

Angel and Julian had said it themselves: Rae was the glue of their little group, the one whose crazy life somehow held everything together. Not the simplest task. Their makeshift family operated within a delicate balance, one that often walked along the razor's edge.

The fact that *she* had been the one to fracture it and disrupt the peace?

It didn't bode well.

How many more times could she just waltz inside and say, "Pack it up, team—there's a new secret cause I want you to risk your lives for"?

Of course, that wasn't entirely accurate. The problems that plagued her plagued them all. It was a universal evil they had been battling. The fight was theirs to share.

But the fact was they were tired of fighting.

They might deny it—she knew for a fact they would all deny it. But the last couple of years had taken a toll. Multiple arrests, betrayals, broken bones, roach-filled motels in the heart of Uganda? It chipped away at all of them, bit by bit. Hell, it chipped away at her, too!

Since before graduation, they had sacrificed everything, done everything that had been asked of them, to get to where they were now. They had gone above and beyond, playing the part of the silent heroes who repeatedly saved the day. But that only threw sharper light onto the obvious:

They were *here* now.

They had new apartments. New significant others. New jobs.

And not to put too fine a point on it, but they had already saved the day. Many times.

The tiny inscribed stone in Rae's pocket suddenly seemed to weigh a million tons. Whatever it turned out to mean, would it be the proverbial straw that broke the camel's back? The little stone that finally smashed through these glass houses and shattered everything they'd been trying to build?

Deep down, did any of them want her to walk back through those doors with another hare-brained adventure up her sleeve?

Deep down, did any of them want her to walk back through those doors at all...?

Oh, come on. Melo-dramatic much, Kerrigan?

"Alrightie. How we doing back there? Feeling brave?"

Quicker than seemed realistically possible, the taxi was back against the curb and Rae looked up in alarm. They were here? *Already?* She gulped loudly and tightened her hands on the straps of her bag.

Well, whatever was going to happen, she wasn't going to have to wait long to find out.

"Oh yeah," she lied, fighting back a wave of nausea, "feeling totally brave." With a silent prayer for strength, she finally pulled open the door.

"Atta girl." Billy grinned, as she planted both feet firmly on the sidewalk.

"Thanks again," she said, casting a nervous glance at the top floor. "I owe you one."

He grinned and twisted around in his seat. "Actually, you owe me much more than that."

She blushed and handed her credit card through the partition.

Poor man. She'd made him drive around the same square mile of space for the last thirty minutes. Truth be told, if he hadn't started prompting her in the last five, there's no telling how many more times they would have circled the block.

"You're a gem." She scrawled her signature, adding on a generous tip.

"Don't mention it." He lifted his hand to wave goodbye. But just before pulling away into traffic, he called out to her once more. "Hey—hon?"

She turned around in surprise. "Yeah?"

He studied her anxious fidgeting for a moment, before his face softened into a smile. "Whatever or whoever it is you're hiding from in there...it's gonna work itself out. You couldn't have screwed up that bad, right?"

Her smile sickened into a pathetic-looking grimace. "You'd be surprised."

He was still chuckling as she trudged her way into the lobby.

"Oh Miss Kerrigan!" Raphael, the cartoonishly-enthusiastic building attendant jumped up the second she walked through the door. "You're back already!"

"Hey, Raph," She offered him a quick one-armed hug, pleased that at least one person in London wasn't angry with her. "Don't they ever give you time off?"

"Please," he scoffed, "this place would fall to pieces without me. But enough about me! I'm so glad to see you! This place is so quiet when you're gone!"

Rae cocked her head to the side. "Pardon me?"

He lowered his voice conspiratorially and flashed her an ostentatious wink. "Well, not to put too fine a point on it, but this building hasn't seen so much drama since old Mrs. Flannery moved out in the seventies. It's like living in a sit-com!"

Yeah...the kind of sit-com that starts out funny and cute before the cast bands together against the troublesome main character and throws her out on her ass so they can have normal lives...

"Well, I'm glad to keep you entertained." She headed into the elevator and pushed the button for the top floor. "Wish me luck."

He beamed back, and she could have sworn she heard him mutter something that sounded suspiciously like, "Team Devon," before the doors closed.

Great. Even the peanut gallery over there has chosen a side.

She watched with growing anxiety as the numbers counted up to her floor, wondering absentmindedly how the strange spectacle that had become her life must look to a passive observer like Raphael. An ever-changing stream of visitors coming and going at all hours of the night. Tears and blood and scrapes and bruises? Not to mention, Victor Mallins' unintentional impersonation of Jack the Ripper showing up at the crack of dawn?

Poor Raphael probably thought they were running some kind of sex club. Or fight club. Or possibly the strangest book club in all the UK.

She tried not to think about it too much as the doors *dinged* and she slowed to a stop.

The horde of angry butterflies in her stomach reached critical mass, but she took a deep breath and forced herself to be calm. Billy-the-cab-driver was right. She was overreacting. This was her home, and no matter what had happened, these were her friends.

With any luck, no one had even noticed she was gone...

"RAE KERRIGAN!"

All the air rushed from Rae's chest with a strangled *yeep*, and she froze in the entryway.

Six angry people were staring back at her.

It was even worse than she had imagined. They were grouped in pairs—Molly and Luke, Angel and Julian—with Devon and Gabriel standing as far away from each other as possible on the ends. It was Molly who had screamed when she came in, so Rae focused all attention on her, carefully avoiding the eyes of the others.

What were they going to do? Trial by fire?

She had to admit, as bad as she'd pictured this moment she hadn't anticipated anything so...public. Her transgression with Gabriel had been private, as was her split with Devon. Now, given the fact that since they were a super-spy crime-fighting team and everything each of them did affected the others, she had expected a certain level of animosity. She had disrupted the harmony of the team, so she deserved some fall-out.

But she had expected it to be silent. Passive aggressive. A dirty look here—a sharp reprimand there. And then it would be finished. Balance would be restored.

She hadn't expected anything like this. The six of them lined up like a firing squad? *Really?*

"Um...hey," she started uncertainly, keeping her eyes firmly on Molly while watching Devon in her periphery all the while. "What are you guys—"

"Where the hell have you been?!" Molly interrupted.

For the first time, Rae glanced curiously at Angel. As the person who had basically talked her into leaving, she would have expected that Angel would have told them she'd be gone.

"I went to see my mom for a few—"

"Yeah, we know you went to Scotland." Molly crossed her arms over her chest and raised a dangerous eyebrow. "I'm talking about *after*."

All the color drained from Rae's face. That same little stone, still burning a hole in her pocket, felt like it was dragging her down through the floorboards, straight into hell.

How could they have possibly known? Did Julian have a vision?

When it became clear that Rae was in no condition to answer, Molly tossed back her hair with a rather dramatic roll of the eyes. "Your mother called. She's been worried sick."

Rae's mouth fell open in confusion. "My mother...?"

Then it suddenly clicked.

Of course! How many times had Mom told her to check in the moment she touched back down in London? She'd done all but write it on Rae's hand. And then to have radio silence?

As a Kerrigan? With their family's history? Radio silence was never a good thing.

She thought guiltily of her cell phone—undoubtedly buried somewhere in the dark recesses of her purse, the battery completely drained. Truth be told, it hadn't crossed her mind for a single moment while she was at Dunnett Head to let anyone know where she was. The idea of direct parental supervision was still something she was getting used to. That and the concept of 'checking in.'

"She called me about five hundred times," Molly continued in a huff, and gestured to the rest of the group. "Each of us. And that's a conservative estimate. Said that you were supposed to have landed two days ago? She thinks you've been freaking kidnapped or murdered or something, Rae! She wanted Carter to activate the Privy Council—"

"No need to activate the Council." Rae raised her hands quickly, a bit fuzzy on what 'activating the Council' would actually mean. "I'm totally fine. No kidnapping. No murder."

Even from across the room, she saw Devon's shoulders relax a bit in relief. She lifted her eyes tentatively to see him, but Molly stepped quickly into her line of sight.

"It's not exactly a stretch for her to have thought that, you know. You're a Kerrigan, Rae. That means no sudden world-changing movements, and absolutely no disappearing off the grid without a trace. Honestly..." Her blue eyes narrowed to dangerous slits. "And you owe me about five hundred rollover minutes on my phone."

Rae nodded quickly, but in spite of her friend's anger she couldn't help but feel immensely relieved. They weren't standing here to confront her. They hadn't come because they knew anything about her time in the Scottish Highlands. They were simply here because they thought she had fallen prey to some tragic, fiery demise.

Kid stuff! That was something she could work with!

A spray of electric blue sparks shot from Molly's hand, setting a nearby rug on fire. "Are you actually *smiling* right now?! Tell me you're not smiling, Rae, or so help me—"

"I'm not smiling," Rae answered quickly, fighting to keep her face clear of emotion as Luke got a glass of water from the kitchen and automatically put out the fire. "I'm sorry, I just..." her eyes flicked over the group, before she dropped them quickly to the floor, "I'm fine. I just forgot to call. Sorry."

For a second, nobody moved.

Then there was a sudden break in the ice, and the room visibly relaxed.

"See—I told you," Angel tossed back her long white hair, "*forgetful*—not *dead*." She turned to Julian with a seductive grin. "So can we go home now? I have a couple rather interesting ideas about how you and I can spend the rest of the afternoon..."

"Where did you go, anyway?" Molly asked in an only slightly less irritated tone. She sank down into an arm chair and threw her legs over the side. "After you left your mom's?"

Rae shifted nervously. "Oh, you know...just driving around..."

Her mind scrambled to come up with a way to explain things further, but fortunately Molly had lost interest in the question almost as soon as she said it, turning instead to talk with Luke, who had successfully doused the flames. Julian flashed her a similar inquisitive glance, his dark eyes searching hers, but then Angel stroked the side of his face and he turned away with a grin, leaving Rae standing in a silent triangle with the last two people in the world she had expected to see.

Devon's eyes were fixed on the wall behind her, refusing to make contact, but Gabriel was glaring at her full-on. Before Rae could say anything to either one of them, he pushed out the door past her, knocking hard into her shoulder on the way.

Angel detached herself from Julian long enough to stare after him with worried eyes. When Rae flashed her a helpless glance, she shrugged and murmured, "We thought you were in serious trouble. It's not like he wouldn't come." Her eyes clouded once more. "But that doesn't mean he has to be happy about it..."

Before Rae even had a chance to process this, Devon picked his jacket up off the kitchen counter and slipped it over his arms. "See you at home, Jules," he said quietly as he headed out.

There was an awkward moment as he passed by Rae, still huddled in the door frame, but when her skin flamed a humiliating shade of crimson, he couldn't help but smile.

"Calm down, Kerrigan. You'll give yourself a heart attack."

She blushed even deeper, but stared up at him with a tentative grin. "I'm just surprised to see you here..."

"What was I going to do? Not come?"

Her shoulders fell with a little sigh, and as much as she'd been dying to see him since the moment she left, she suddenly found it very hard to meet his gaze. "I just thought you might want to have a little—"

"Rae." He dropped his voice several octaves, so that no matter the casually prying eyes in the kitchen, they were the only two people who could hear. "I was clear that night in the park. You know exactly how I feel about you. Of course I came." Without seeming to think about it, he leaned a few inches forward, staring deep into her eyes. But as quickly as it had happened, he remembered himself and backed away. "I'm just happy you're alright," he said formally, clearing his throat and pulling open the door. "See you around, Kerrigan. Keep your phone on."

See you around, Kerrigan.

A poor substitute for a Devon Wardell kiss goodnight, but who was she to complain?

He slipped into his tatù and was down the stairs before she could even turn around to say goodbye. It was probably for the best, as she was having a rather impossible time controlling her face right now. The corners of her eyes stung with forbidden tears, and she turned around before anyone could else see, hiding them under the guise of picking up her purse.

While that might have been enough to fool Luke and Angel, Molly and Julian saw through it at once. They let her cross to her room without question, though; either too frustrated, too polite, or too merciful to confront her with anything right then.

She slipped inside, shut the door behind her, and collapsed on the bed, feeling as though the entire world had flipped on its head.

How had everything gotten so complicated so quickly? How had she let things get so messed up? A few stray tears spilled down her cheeks and she muffled a sob in her pillow.

In what universe would Devon not kiss her goodnight?

As if to further torment her, the mysterious little stone rolled out of her purse and came to a stop against her shoulder. She picked it up and turned it over again with a frown, tracing her fingers over the inscription.

Personal dramas aside, the others needed to know about this. The Council needed to have the final piece. There were urgent things that needed to be done, except...

She jerked the blanket up over her head.

...except, until she could go outside without crying, all that would just have to wait.

Chapter 2

It took forever to fall asleep that night and once she did, Rae kept tossing and turning with the same repeating dream.

It started out simply enough...

She was walking through the grounds of Guilder. School friends and faculty drifted in and out, each one pointing her towards the Oratory with strange, solemn faces. She followed along obediently, not quite scared, but worried over what could be waiting inside. Pushing open the large entrance door, she walked down the black and white marbled hallway to the large room, coming to a stop in the center of it beneath the high, domed ceilings.

Every seat in the room was full, just like the day of her graduation performance. Each person sat on the edge of their chair, every eye trained on her.

She rotated slowly around as a series of nervous chills ran up her back. What was she doing here? Why had they brought her? What the heck was everyone waiting for?

Then Devon walked purposefully towards her from across the other side of room. He'd come from one of the carved wooden walls, a hidden door from the Privy Council tunnels.

Her body relaxed, and she brightened with a hopeful smile. If Devon was here it couldn't be anything too terrible, could it? He'd never let anything happen to her if it was in his control.

Except Devon's face looked just as grave as the others.

Her smile faded the closer he got, and by the time he was standing in front of her she was bracing herself for whatever was to come. "Dev, what is it? What's going on?"

His blue eyes stared intently into hers, before he answered in a strange voice; a voice that was too low and distant to be his own.

"I'm sorry, Rae. I didn't know..." He pressed something cold into her hands and began walking away.

"Wait! What are you talking about!? What didn't you know?!" She tried to run after him, but her feet were rooted to the ground, unable to move. "Devon—wait!"

Nevertheless, even as she called to him, he faded into the mist at the other side of the room. Another man walked out in his place; a tall man with thick muscles and a broad chest, bright blue eyes and short, curly hair. He came to a sudden stop in front of her, and stared just as intently as Devon had.

Her own memories were corrupted with age, but there was not a shadow of doubt in her heart as to who he was.

"Dad?"

His eyes warmed, but his face was stern. "There's no time, Rae. Get ready!"

There was a metallic scrape, and she looked down with a start. It was then that she realized he was holding the same thing Devon had handed to her. A knife.

He pulled it slowly from its sheath, and her body chilled. Acting on instinct, she reached down and pulled out her own, backing away as he took a step towards her.

"Are you really going to do this?" she whispered, her eyes flickering to the screaming, cheering crowd. "Are you really going to fight your own daughter?"

But Simon's eyes weren't on Rae. They were focused on something just behind her back. Something coming in fast.

"Rae—look out!"

She whirled around, but by that time it was already too late. The silver handle of a knife stuck out three inches from her stomach, and her shirt soaked slowly through with blood. In a daze, she lifted her head to see the person standing in front of her—his hands still gripping the handle. Her eyes dilated in anticipation as he slowly removed his hood.

Then he ripped out the knife and she fell to her knees with a gasp.

"No!" she cried. "It's—"

With a half-strangled shriek, Rae bolted up in bed, clutching her stomach where the knife had been just moments before. Her fingers pressed against her skin as she fought to remember the face of the man. It was someone she had seen before.

Someone she knew very well...

But just like a dream, the harder she tried to remember the faster it slipped from her.

All that was left was a panting girl, a mess of tangled sheets, and a screeching alarm clock she hadn't remembered setting.

Instead of simply silencing it, she fired a strategic bolt of lightning—Molly-style—and shattered the thing against the far wall. It was six a.m.; far too early for her taste, but she had made a vital decision last night before going to sleep. That decision required her to be out of the house before anyone realized what was going on.

Quiet as a mouse she got up, conjured herself some fresh clothes, and took a steadying look in the mirror. Lifting her shirt above her stomach, she turned this way and that.

See? Nothing there. Just a dream.

But a nagging feeling of dread followed her about as she circled through the room, pulling out clothes and toiletries and throwing them onto the bed. When she had gathered a big enough pile, she conjured herself two suitcases and stuffed everything inside. She was going on a little trip today. One where she intended to find out some serious answers.

Packed and ready faster than she thought it would take, she double-checked her phone's battery that she charged the night before. It was good to go. Glancing once at her half-hearted attempted to make her bed, she crept from her bedroom and shut the door silently behind her.

Try as she might to shake it, her mind was still stuck on the dream. It wasn't the first time she'd had it, but it was definitely the most vivid time, leaving her with a sickening feeling she couldn't explain.

Who was the man who'd stabbed her? And why had her father warned her it was coming?

Furthermore, why had—

"Devon!" she half-whispered, half-hissed in surprise. She stopped short when saw him standing in the kitchen behind her, silently watching her with sapphire eyes. He was dressed in workout shorts and a black tank, the kind she secretly loved to see him wear. While he reclined casually against the counter, his posture seemed a little too intentionally relaxed to be realistic. He was as startled to see her as she was to see him.

"Sorry," she gasped, putting her hand to her chest. "You scared me."

"I'm surprised you didn't hear me," he said lightly, eyes flickering over her bags. "I thought you said you usually used my fennec tatù as your default."

"Yeah," she stammered, tucking her hair nervously behind her ears, "I usually do..." In all honesty, she was surprised to realize she hadn't been. Most of the time, she chose what ink she wanted to slip into—but on rare occasions, occasions when she needed it the most—her body switched tatùs involuntarily.

What puzzled her now wasn't that her body had made the switch. It was that it had switched into Charles' ability.

The ability to heal.

Without stopping to think about it, her hands drifted down to her stomach.

"What's wrong?"

Her head snapped up to attention. Devon was standing now, studying her odd position with a concern that he was either unable or unwilling to hide. Their eyes met for the briefest moment before she quickly changed the subject. "Why are you here?"

It came out a little sharper than she had intended, but perhaps it was for the best. They both snapped out of their momentary trance, and Devon cleared his throat.

"I'm meeting Luke; we're supposed to go to the gym. We thought we'd get an early start before—"

His voice cut off in sudden, incriminating panic, and Rae realized the words he had been going to say.

'Before anybody else woke up.'

She and Devon might have broken up, but that didn't mean that they stopped thinking the same way. Social retreats were best done at early dawn while everyone else was sleeping.

"What's with the bags?" he deflected, feeling a little sheepish that he'd let something slip.

Rae glanced down where they sat on either side of her feet. "Oh, I'm just—"

"Well, good morning!" Molly threw open the door to her bedroom, looking considerably more relaxed than she had the previous evening. She leaned against the frame, wearing a long bathrobe, and offered each one of them a bright, oblivious smile.

A second later, she remembered their current situation and turned an off-shade of puce.

"Oh...sorry, I didn't—"

"Hey man," Luke breezed past her, casually alleviating the sudden tension, "you ready to hit the weights?"

"Yeah, absolutely." Devon picked up his gear, but glanced again at Rae's suitcases and paused. "I was just..."

Molly beat him to it. "Where the hell do you think you're going *now*?"

Rae flushed, and spoke without thinking. "I'm going to New York."

"New York?" Devon repeated with a slight frown. His eyes flickered between his gym bag and her suitcases, like he was trying to decide which way to go.

"New York City?" Molly asked a little more seriously. "What's happened?" Before Rae could even answer, she disappeared into her room and began rummaging around in her closet. She appeared a moment later with an empty suitcase of her own, into which she began throwing random pieces of clothing. "Well, how long do you think we're going to be gone?" she asked, sweeping her hair up into a long red ponytail as she worked. "We can text Julian and pick him up along the way—"

"*I'm* going to New York," Rae repeated, stressing the isolation. "Just me."

Molly paused in her frantic packing, looking utterly bewildered, while Devon set his bag slowly on the floor. "Why wouldn't we...?" Molly trailed off uncertainly, before shaking her head. "Don't be stupid, so you guys are having a fight. So what? You'll get past it. Of course we're coming with—"

"I'm going to New York to see my uncle," Rae cut her off. "There's no life or death situation, there's no monstrous game afoot. I'm just...going to visit my uncle and aunt." She was surprised by how easily the story rolled off her tongue. It wasn't like she was exactly lying. She was indeed going to visit her uncle in New York.

There was just a bit more to it than that.

"Oh, well..." Molly glanced down at her half-packed bag, before her eyes drifted up to Luke. "Do you want a travelling companion, or...?"

"No, no it's fine," Rae assured her quickly. "I've been meaning to go for a long time, but there's always too much stuff going on. But now Cromfield's gone, and everything is just..." she avoided Devon's eyes, "...over."

"I'd still totally go with you if you wanted—"

"It's cool, Molls." Rae flashed her a quick smile before picking up the bags and heading to the door. "I'll be back in a few days. A week tops." She sucked in a quick breath and put on a brave face, hating to be lying to her friends, even if it was only a little white lie. "See you... everyone."

"Okay, well...'bye then." Molly raised a hand in a tentative wave, while Luke did the same thing behind her. "Text me when you get there?"

"I will. Bye." As she headed out the door, she glanced back at Devon without meaning to. He was still watching her with that same worried look. *He knows me too well. He knows something's going on.* Flashing a deliberately casual smile, she nodded to him as well. "See you, Dev."

It wasn't until she'd already shut the door behind her that she heard him answer.

"...See you."

Rae spent most of the flight to New York with her nose buried in some nonsense book she had gotten at the airport. She knew enough about international travel to know that if you were travelling alone—someone, didn't matter who, but *someone*— would always try to talk to you. And while that may be an amusing way to pass the time for some people, she simply didn't have the energy. Or the time. She would be landing in just a few short hours, and still had to come up with a way to pry sensitive information out of her uncle.

"Miss? Another soft drink?"

Rae flipped a page in the book, trying to look busy as the young man behind her leaned forward with interest to get a better look. "Yes, thank you."

"Here you are." The woman set it down with a kind smile before leaning closer. "And, Miss...your book is upside-down."

With a look of extreme mortification, Rae sank lower in her seat and turned it back the right way. "Thanks."

Five hours later, she was no closer to coming up with a tactic to combat her uncle, but was now suddenly out of time. She hopped into a cab at the airport and headed straight to her aunt and uncle's house in the middle of the city.

Cabs in New York were nothing like cabs in London, she realized as she pressed her nose against the window and watched the commotion.

Instead of her serene English streets, there was a dissonant symphony of rapid honking and profanity. Instead of her charming little break-up park lined with antique benches and miniature roses...there was a broken- down hot dog stand and a pair of stolen bicycle wheels.

Still...home sweet home, in a way. It was good to be back.

As fate would have it, she pulled up at the house just as Uncle Argyle and Aunt Linda were leaving it. King Arthur, her aunt's prized cat, was wedged in a carrying case beneath Linda's arm.

"Is that...?" Linda shoved the case into Argyle's chest and raced down the steps, her arms raised for a huge hug. "Is that my Rae?! Honey, I didn't even recognize you! Come here!"

Before Rae could say a word, she'd been pulled into her aunt's famous bone-crushing embrace. For the second time that day, her body slipped into Charles' ability. At least this time she understood the reason why.

"Hi, Aunt Linda," she gasped, mentally checking to make sure all her vertebrae were intact.

"Oh, sweetheart! You look all grown up! I didn't even recognize you!" Linda twisted around and squawked in Argyle's direction. "I didn't even recognize her!"

"Yes, darling, I heard you the first two times." Argyle trotted down the steps and set the cat in the backseat of their car. "Rae, it's so good to see you. All is well, I hope. We weren't expecting a visit..." His voice trailed off and he studied her face curiously.

While Linda remained cheerfully oblivious, he looked at his niece with a bit more caution. He alone knew the well-deserved implications behind her last name. He alone knew that 'surprise visits' were seldom a good thing.

Rae pulled back a bit nervously, but smiled with false cheer. "Yeah, well, I'd saved up some vacation days at work and decided to hop on a plane and surprise you!"

Linda clapped her hands. "Argyle, isn't that wonderful! She'd saved up some vacation days at work and decided to—"

Argyle chuckled softly and put an arm around his wife's shoulders. "Yes, dear. I heard her the first time." He glanced at the black town car idling beside the curb. "We were just on our way to the vet's. Apparently Arthur is feeling...depressed, and urgent medical care is required."

Rae looked back and forth between them and stifled a smile. The royal treatment of the family cat had always been a fervent insistence of her aunt's, and the bane of her uncle's existence.

"He's...depressed?" she repeated curiously. "How can you tell?"

A shadow passed over Argyle's face and he rolled his eyes to the heavens. "The same question I've been asking for three days—"

"He's just not feeling like himself," Linda cooed, sticking her fingers through the case. "Ever since they closed down the Picasso gallery at the Met, he's been inconsolable."

Rae couldn't tell if she was joking. Then again, her aunt *never* joked about the cat. She decided to act cautiously. "Well, that's enough to make anyone go to the vet. You two run along. I'll just show myself in. I could use some sleep anyway."

"Are you sure, dear?" Linda looked torn. "You just got here, I don't want to miss out on any time with you, and I certainly don't want you to be all alone—"

"Tell you what," Rae proposed slyly. "Why doesn't Uncle Argyle stay with me? You can take King Arthur to the vet, and we can have some dinner ready for when you get home." When her aunt wavered, she pressed her luck still further. "I'm sure Arthur would rather go with you than Uncle Argyle anyway," she said in a conspiratorial voice. "You are his favorite..."

Linda nodded whole-heartedly. "Too true, dear, too true. In that case, we'll be back in less than an hour. Cupboards are stocked. You two have fun!" She put Arthur in the front seat and hopped into car without another word, waving out the window as Rae and her uncle stood on the curb—fixed smiles on their faces.

"So you want to tell me what this little visit is about?" he asked, still waving as Linda pulled around the corner.

Rae grinned at the departing car. "Funny you should ask. You and I need to have a little talk about my dad..."

Chapter 3

"Your father," Uncle Argyle began wearily as he pulled various ingredients from the cabinets to start making dinner. "As I recall, you came here for Christmas not long ago and already asked me all about your father. I'm not sure what else I can tell you."

Rae leaned against the kitchen counter with her hands on her hips. "You can tell me if you trusted him."

Argyle paused, hands frozen in the refrigerator, before he pulled out a slab of cheese. "You know I did, Rae," he sighed, "we all did. None of us saw it coming."

She scurried around the counter to get the cutting board and a knife. "Saw *what* coming, exactly? That's why I'm here, Uncle. My entire life, all I've ever gotten is a series of partial answers and vague half-truths. I need someone to just sit down and tell me the whole story. No more cryptic dodges. Just the truth. I think you're the only one who can." The words came out with a bit more passion than she'd intended, probably a result of her recent internal rant about precisely that frustration.

Argyle considered her carefully over his reading glasses before pouring himself a glass of wine. "The truth is..." he took a deep sip, "the truth is that I believed in him. He inspired me. He inspired a lot of us. And it wasn't just that he had an eloquent way of talking; there was this...this quality about him. An aura, if you will. It made him rather irresistible."

Rae hung on every word. So absorbed was she, that she didn't realized she had stopped slicing until her uncle motioned for her to continue.

"In school, he was well-liked and admired. Perhaps not by all the faculty, and there were a few students who never quite warmed to him. Your boyfriend's father, for one."

Rae almost sliced right through her finger. "What? Dean Wardell knew my dad?"

"You've been dating his son for how many years, and you still call him *Dean* Wardell?"

Rae flushed beet-red, and returned to the cheese. "For your information, the man and I never really warmed to each other either." Her cheeks flushed even hotter. "That, and I'm no longer dating his son."

Argyle frowned over his wine. "What was that last part?"

"Nothing." Rae cleared her throat quickly and moved on. "You were saying?"

"Yes, well, the teachers at Guilder soon took a great interest in the 'propaganda' your father was preaching. Freedom to use our powers openly in the world. Refusal to hide. While most of them dismissed it as the vigor of youth, news of it soon spread up the ladder to the higher-ups actually running the school."

"And from the higher ups...to the Privy Council," Rae surmised. "Lanford was one of those teachers spreading it, wasn't he?"

Argyle nodded. "Simon was one of the only ones in his year *not* to be offered a job with the Council after graduation. Not before, like you had, nor after he graduated. His peers couldn't understand it. Not only was he one of the best and the brightest, but his tatù was powerful and unlike anything they had ever seen. I remember your mother being devastated that he wouldn't be joining her and her friend Jennifer at the agency. But I digress... I imagine it's what Simon did after school that's of greatest interest to you."

Simon had worked for the Privy Council, but it had been a secret. Rae was sure of it. Maybe he'd left or been fired. Maybe he'd started the Xavier Knights or joined up with them. It didn't matter at this moment. Argyle wouldn't know. She nodded slowly, and watched her uncle's face for any hidden clues that might lie there.

Truth be told, she wasn't looking for any one thing in particular. There wasn't a specific anecdote she was waiting to uncover. She simply wanted to understand the man.

Her entire life, she'd been unable to reconcile it.

So he'd had affairs—lots of men do. Of course, they didn't do it as a genetic experiment to try to create a hybrid super-baby, but hey—semantics.

So he'd created a secret society—she didn't exactly disagree with their doctrine. While the extremist tendencies were obviously downright wrong, the premise of what the HOC stood for wasn't too far away from things she believed herself. She didn't like to hide her gift. She didn't like the fact that, as a hybrid, she was openly reviled even within her world. And she certainly didn't understand how every person with ink was banned from sharing the secret even with family.

After decades of marriage, Aunt Linda still had no idea what kind of school Argyle had attended for a short while. She had no idea what Rae had been doing for the last few years, and as far as Rae knew, Linda believed she 'worked in sales.' Whatever that was supposed to mean.

How could Argyle keep something like that from her? Something as fundamental as what he was—his family and bloodline? How could Devon's mom have no idea how her son spent his days? How could Molly's mom? How had it become a standard that everyone was simply okay with?

And the fact that the PC even had the gall to tell people who they were allowed to love?!

Now I'm digressing...

But the fact remained her mother had still fallen in love with this man. How had this charming school boy turned into the Simon Kerrigan monster she knew today?

Rae brought herself back to the present and began plating grapes with the cheese. "All I know is that my mom was tasked with spying on him. That he was on the Privy Council's most wanted list as enemy number one."

Argyle sighed. "He was placed there after it was suspected that he murdered his parents."

That. How could her mother have fallen in love with *that*? How was anyone capable of *that*?

"Do you think he did it?" Rae asked quietly, peeking up through her lashes to see her uncle's face. The second she did, she almost wished she hadn't.

He had gone from almost wistfully nostalgic to abruptly sad. He downed the wine in another gulp and started sprinkling seasoning on a plate of steamed vegetables.

"All the evidence says that he did," he said quietly. "The Privy Council ran an official investigation. I remember your mother studying the case report herself. She said it was black and white. Simon was guilty."

Rae's shoulders fell with a little sigh. She hadn't even realized she'd been holding her breath. Holding out hope was more like it. That this heinous crime didn't belong in her family. That there had been some kind of mistake. "I barely remember Grandpa P and Nanny K," she murmured. "I'd only seen pictures of them." Her father rarely spoke of them, from what she could remember. Her six-year-old self didn't have much family stuff to go on except what Argyle and Linda had taught her in the years following.

Argyle chuckled, "I forgot you used to call them that."

Rae looked up curiously. "What else would I call them?"

"Well, I always knew them as Peter and Katerina. Their given Russian names."

Rae sliced through her finger.

"RAE!"

She looked down in surprise to see a small geyser of blood gushing over the counter. While Argyle raced forward with a towel, she lifted the plate of cheese out of the way with almost robotic disinterest. Truth be told, she was so distracted she hardly felt the pain.

Grandpa P and Nanny K...Peter and Katerina.

They were the same people.

Her grandparents.

Her mind flashed back to the words from her father's letter. 'The Privy Council was not always so spotless and forthcoming as they would have people believe. You need proof, ask Peter and Katerina...'

But what the hell did that mean? Why would he point her attention to the very people he'd killed? What on earth did he think that was going to prove against the Council?

"Earth to Rae! Are you even listening?!"

She snapped back to attention to find her uncle holding a towel firmly over her finger with one hand, while the other reached for the phone.

"Just hang on, sweetie; I'm going to call the family doctor. He makes house calls—"

"Uncle," she pulled away, "I'm fine. Look. Already healed."

Maybe she should just stick to Charles' tatù. From the way things were going, she'd probably need it.

She watched her uncle's eyes widen in shock just as the front door pushed open. As the sharp clang of stilettos and the jingle of a cat collar echoed down the hardwood floors, she and Argyle shot each other a panicked look. As if they'd rehearsed it, she conjured a sponge to wipe the remaining blood of the counter while he threw the soiled towel in the trash. They'd just finished when Linda came bursting through the door, King Arthur safely in her arms.

"Well, Dr. Millstone seems to think he's going to pull through." Her eyes swept the disheveled kitchen with a faint smile. "And I can see you two decided on cheese, grapes, and vegetables for dinner."

As one, Rae and Argyle stared guiltily around the kitchen. They'd been so wrapped up in their conversation they realized they didn't quite have a game plan for dinner.

"How about I order Chinese?" Linda suggested, giving each an indulgent grin.

"Sounds perfect, dear," Argyle said quickly. "I'll go upstairs and clean up."

As he swept from the kitchen, Rae couldn't help but think that he was not only eager to get away from his inexplicably durable niece, but also from her line of questioning. It had clearly taken him down a side-street of memory lane, where he wasn't too keen to go.

She understood the feeling. As she helped her aunt pick up around the kitchen and mimed the smiles of polite conversation, she felt as though her head was a million miles away. She had come to New York looking for answers, but as usual all she'd gotten were more questions.

But at least this time will be different, she thought with determination. *This time I can take matters into my own hands.*

Because, while she might have a whole host of new mysteries to solve, her conversation with Argyle had given her something else, too.

A pair of names. A place to start digging.

Well how about it, Dad...game on!

"I just don't understand," Aunt Linda said with a frown, watching as Rae shoved handfuls of bacon and biscuits into her mouth. "You've never shown the slightest interest in going to the library before..."

Rae struggled to swallow, washing everything down with a huge swig of coffee. "What are you talking about? I've always loved the library."

It wasn't true. She suspected her aunt knew this.

Sure enough, Linda raised her eyebrows in disbelief. "The New York Public Library? Do you even know where it is?"

Rae faltered for a second. How was it that in all her years of collecting, she'd never gotten some sort of map tatù?

"Of course I know where it is," she countered, meeting her aunt's sly grin with an even slyer grin of her own. "I mean...I have a friend who knows where it is."

"Uh-huh." Her aunt chuckled. "And would this friend happen to be whatever taxi driver you hail down first?"

"Now you're catching on! Who needs a map in New York when we've all been blessed to live in the land of Yellow Cab?" She leapt up from the table and kissed her aunt swiftly on the cheek before heading out the door. "I'll be back for dinner!"

Aunt Linda was most certainly right. Rae wasn't sure she had ever set foot in the library, save for the occasional class field trip, and she was surprised by how huge it was when she stepped inside.

In all honesty, all she'd really wanted was a computer and a safe place to research away from her aunt and uncle's prying eyes. At this rate the library seemed like overkill. She should have just stepped into a Starbucks. Of course, they didn't come with complimentary laptops...

As she took a seat and logged in using the library code, she wondered where it was she was supposed to start. 'Peter and Katerina Kerrigan.' Maybe the names were more common than she thought. She bit her lip nervously as she typed them into the search engine, bracing herself for how many results she might find.

As it turned out, there weren't a lot. She browsed through the first dozen or so, eliminating them as possibilities, until finally something looked familiar.

Aha! Bingo!

She clicked on the article and leaned forward to read:

'Russian Couple Found Dead'

'Peter and Katerina Kerrigan were found dead in their home today; the result of what police are now officially ruling a homicide. Initial reports state that both Mr. and Mrs. Kerrigan died of massive blood loss after being shot in the chest. While no suspects are being listed at this time, it's possible that their deaths were the result of a home invasion gone wrong. They are survived by their son, Simon Kerrigan, who currently resides in London.'

Rae sat back in her chair with a sigh. A thought crossed her mind: *Bet Kraigan would love this...*

However, as strange as it was to find the official report, it offered no further clues as to why Simon had directed Rae to look them up. Killed by guns in their home? Not exactly the Privy Council's style, if that's what he was getting at. Then again, it wasn't exactly his style either. The only person with ink she'd ever known to use a gun was Kraigan, and bless his heart, seeing as he wasn't born then, this was one of the few crimes Rae could say with certainty her half-brother did not commit.

But that still begged the question: Why would her father direct her here? Why have her look into the deaths of her grandparents? Was Simon trying to say he didn't do it? That he was framed as some part of a huge cover-up?

She clicked around for a while longer, but was unable to come up with any more leads. At this point, she hadn't really expected to. The information she needed wasn't going to be found here at a library in New York. No, if she really wanted to get the answers she needed, she'd have to go right to the source. And that meant stopping by a place she'd rather avoid at the moment.

The Privy Council.

No sooner had she thought the words than her phone buzzed in her pocket. She extracted it with a small smile, not bothering to even look at the Caller ID.

"Hey Jules."

"So you're coming back home? That was a quick visit."

She stifled a grin, thrilled that he was still talking to her. She was worried that she might get the silent treatment for a while longer out of loyalty to Devon. "Mind your own business, psychic."

He chuckled softly. "Don't you think I'm trying? Do you have any idea how hard it is to explain when my eyes go blank and I mutter the word 'Rae' when I'm with Angel? It always seems to happen at the most inopportune times..."

Now it was Rae's turn to laugh. "Sorry to intrude." Her breath caught suddenly in her chest, and she found herself bowing her head in shame. "Jules...I'm sorry about a lot of things."

There was a brief pause, filled with a soft rustling sound. She could just picture him shifting his weight uneasily as he tapped on the side of the phone.

"It's none of my business," he answered. But it was stiff. Way more stiff than was normal.

"I never meant to hurt him," her voice dropped to a whisper. "I would never do anything to hurt him. I just...made a mistake."

Julian sighed. "Hey, we all make mistakes. There's no judgement coming from me."

Rae's eyes teared up with gratitude, but she shook her head. "You don't have to say that. I know how the two of you are. Like brothers. If you want to, like, throw stuff and sharpie me out of all our pictures together...I'd completely understand."

He laughed again. "Hey, he might be a brother to me, but I also think of you as a sister. You two are going to work it out—I know it. Just...give it some time."

Rae nodded, trying to keep herself from crying right there in the New York Public Library. "Is that my psychic telling me? Or my friend?"

"Your friend," he snickered. "I'm not reading that future for you. You're going to have to figure it out on your own."

"Fair enough." She grinned, suddenly excited to be going home—to her real home. "Well, I'll see you tomorrow I guess. I'll try to book something for the morning—"

She cut off suddenly as she realized her mistake.

The second she'd imagined going back, she unintentionally imagined exactly what she was going to do when she got there. Needless to say...it wasn't the kind of thing to go unnoticed.

"Rae Kerrigan!"

She paled. "Gotta go, Jules! Bye!"

"Don't you dare hang up this phone!" he yelled. "Explain yourself!"

She glanced nervously around the library, worried people might hear. "Explain...what?" she stalled, trying to figure out a way to get out of it.

"Explain why the hell I just saw you trying to break into the Privy Council! *Again!*"

She bit her lip. No real excuses could explain away that. And he saw all of it in just one second? He was getting too talented at reading the future for his own good.

Then again, since he'd already seen it happening...

"So," she began fishing, "how exactly did you see me accomplishing this master break-in?"

"Oh no," he cut her off sharply, "you are *not* doing this to me again! You are *not* roping me into this! Another break-in, Rae? We *just* got offered our old jobs back!"

"I'm not roping you into anything, Julian." She smiled. "You were the one who had the vision, not me. Did you see yourself there?"

There was another pause, after which Julian sounded increasingly unhappy.

"It's...unclear."

She fought back a grin, but then sobered. They may banter about it back and forth, but this time wasn't going to be like the others. This was her father, her family, her answers she needed to find. If she was indeed going to be infiltrating the PC to find those answers, she would most definitely be doing it alone. Julian would not be coming with her.

"It's not unclear at all," she said decisively. "With Cromfield underground, we're taking a break on the whole team-crime-fighting thing. And even if we weren't, this isn't one of our typical missions, Jules. This is something I need to do alone."

"What?" He sounded both frustrated and concerned. "What do you need to do alone? What is it you aren't telling me?"

"Julian, don't—"

"Don't tell me not to worry about it, because I already saw it happening. And don't tell me that it's 'something you have to do alone,' because you're one of my best friends in the world, Rae, and I love you like family. Whatever it is, we're in it together. So just tell me."

Sitting in a library halfway around the world, Rae drummed her fingers nervously on the table and tried to decide what to do.

Julian wasn't the problem. She would trust Julian with anything—even her life. She could trust him with this. Except...

This was exactly the sort of thing she decided she wasn't going to do.

Her fight. Her problem. Her answers. Right? No need to go dragging all her friends into it?

"Rae. Stop trying to complicate things with your damn over-analysis and just tell me," he interrupted her muddled train of thought. "I'll end up seeing it anyway, so you might as well just let me know."

"Okay, fine," she surrendered, unable to combat the obvious logic in his threat. "But Julian, there's one condition. And this is something you have to swear to stick to no matter what..."

"Okay," he sounded uneasy, "what is it?"

She took a deep breath and let it out slowly. "You absolutely cannot tell Devon."

Chapter 4

Julian stood waiting for Rae at the airport the next afternoon, nervous and tense. He wore a jacket with the collar flipped up, and heavily-tinted sunglasses that still didn't quite hide the fact that his eyes were darting anxiously around the terminal. At first, Rae figured he was worried he might have an unexpected vision. It took her only a second to realize she was seeing five years of psychic neurosis coming into play.

"Very slick," she complimented as she came to a stop in front of him, striking a sarcastic pose. "And just who may I ask do you think would be following you?"

"What are you talking about?" He fidgeted guiltily. "I'm not...No, this isn't—"

"You've just taken to impersonating the KGB for fun?"

He took off his glasses so she could see his scowl. "Cute. Come on; let's just get your bags so we can get out of here." Without another word, he began crossing the terminal in strides so long she struggled to keep pace with him without slipping into a tatù.

Ironically it reminded Rae of her return to Guilder after her first summer away. She'd been following Devon then. She pushed the thought aside. "Seriously, what is *with* you?" she asked with a grin, tugging on his coat to get him to slow his crazy pace.

"Nothing, I just..." His eyes tightened. "I just don't like sneaking around like this behind Devon's back. I don't like lying to him."

Rae bowed her head and hastened to check her emotions. She didn't like it any more than he did, but there were good reasons they were keeping Devon in the dark. "What did you tell him?" she asked quietly.

Julian's shoulders fell in a quick sigh. "I told him I was going rock climbing."

There was a pause. Then Rae burst into laughter.

A family parted curiously around them as she struggled to get herself under control. Under the circumstances, it was rather hard to do.

The furious look on Julian's face wasn't helping much.

"Well," she finally gasped, "you can take comfort in the fact that you barely lied to him at all. That is, without a doubt, the worst lie I've ever heard. It scarcely counts."

Julian's dark eyes narrowed. "You try coming up with something then."

"Oh, I don't know, how about, 'I'm going to see my girlfriend.' Or something around those lines?"

A look of awed simplicity washed over his face, though he was quick to hide it under a mask of impatience. "Let's just go." He tugged her arm and rushed her along. "I'm double-parked."

She allowed herself to be towed to the car, all the while muttering a constant stream of easy substitutes to his pathetic attempt at trickery.

"...going out to lunch...heading to the gym to work out...going to see a movie..."

"Shut up."

"...going to re-read my manual on how to be a spy..."

"SHUT UP, Kerrigan!"

When they finally got back to their part of the city forty-five minutes later, Rae was surprised when Julian bypassed their street altogether, and instead took her to a small diner tucked away behind an industrial warehouse she had never noticed before. She got out of the car in silence and followed him in, sliding obediently into the booth. She smiled politely as the waitress set down their menus, but the second the woman was gone she looked up curiously, waiting for him to speak.

"You're going to have to give me a good reason." As was his custom, Julian spoke quietly but she found herself hanging onto every word. "I know we went over it on the phone," he continued, "but I need to hear it again. In person. Why is it that we aren't telling anyone about this? In particular, why are we keeping it from Devon?"

Rae bit her lip for a second as she thought about it. When she finally looked back up, she knew her face was grim. "Do you remember when Devon jumped off the cliff in Scotland?"

Julian frowned thoughtfully. "When he flew back out?"

Rae shook her head a fraction of an inch and stared intently into his eyes. "I'm asking if you remember when he jumped in..."

A charged silence hung between them, then Julian bowed his head and nodded.

Rae had been thinking about this particular problem the entire flight. There was an old saying, 'I am my beloved's and my beloved is mine.' Devon and Rae might have had a fight. Might have veered off-course. Might have even technically broken up. But nothing had really changed. Nothing ever would. He had hurled his body off of a cliff for her without a second thought, knowing full well he would be dashed to death against the rocks. The second that she needed help—the second her well-being was at stake—he'd made the final sacrifice; offering up every last bit of himself so that she might be safe.,

And what was more, he would do it again in a heartbeat.

In the tumultuous saga that was their lives, one thing remained constant: she was always getting into trouble, and he was always risking his life to save her.

They'd made both a professional and personal career of playing with fire; only, Devon was the only one who could get burned. And as the years went by, it was getting easier and easier to see the scars.

But not this time. This time, he would stay safe. This time, he would get away unscathed. Rae had made a vow that she would keep that promise.

And the only way for that to happen was if he didn't know anything was happening.

"He's happy," Rae said quietly. "He's returned to London, back working with the Privy Council, nothing terrible or life-threatening is on the horizon. He's *happy*," she repeated, as if to reaffirm it to herself. "I'm not going to take all that away because my dead father sent me a letter a decade and a half ago."

Julian stared at her for a long time. Long enough that the waitress delivered their coffee and disappeared back into the shadows without a trace. If it had been anyone else, it would have made Rae completely uncomfortable, but she and Julian had always been different. More natural. They could read each other without the pomp and circumstance inherent with most other people. Some days, they could read each other better than they could read themselves.

It was for this reason that Rae found herself holding her breath—waiting for whatever was going to happen next.

"I won't tell him," he said slowly, weighing each word before letting it go. "And I won't leave you alone in this either. We're doing it together, step by step."

"Jules—"

"Do not argue with me."

Something about his tone silenced her and she dropped her gaze with a small nod. When she glanced back up, he was still staring at her, although there was something different now in his gaze.

Something appraising.

Before she could figure out what it was, he pushed to his feet and slipped his coat back over his shoulders, rummaging around in his pocket and dropping some bills on the table.

"You may have some valid points, Rae, but you're wrong about one thing." His bright clairvoyant eyes rested on her for a second more. "He's not happy."

Then he left the diner.

The next day, Rae woke at the crack of dawn, jet-lagged to the point of delirium, but bursting with excitement to start the first phase of her plan. She couldn't lie: she loved the job that the PC offered her, except this was even better. *Focus, Rae. What's the plan?*

Step one: Guilder.

Slipping into what was quickly becoming her unofficial favorite tatù, she conjured herself a pair of sleek black running tights and a matching black camisole. She slicked her hair back into a long, tumbling ponytail and even added a touch of dark lipstick to complete the look.

It was something that Molly would call 'athletic chic' were she to see it.

Pleased with her efforts, Rae brushed her teeth, sprayed on a spritz of perfume, and sailed out the door before anyone was the wiser. Moments later, her feet hit the pavement.

Jogging had never really been her thing; anyone who knew her could tell you that. Even during the time she was training at Guilder, she and Molly would often shirk their runs under the guise of doing more 'research,' a spirited activity that secretly translated to pancake breakfasts. Same with when she started training with the Privy Council.

But she and Julian needed a cover. He couldn't be relied upon to spin consistent stories that Devon would believe, and she didn't want to risk the wrath of his hot-tempered girlfriend for dominating all his time. They'd need a go-to excuse for why they would be out of their respective homes so often and spending so much time alone together.

Rae had decided this excuse would be jogging.

Unfortunately, she'd also decided that—in honor of Julian—it would be jogging sans tatù.

It was an idea that looked great on paper, but after only a few minutes of slugging away in the park her body rebelled and she felt the need to cheat.

Who would ever know, right? She'd still move at Julian's normal pace; she'd just have a secret safety net.

The second she slipped into Devon's tatù, the relief was instantaneous. Gone were the muscle cramps and the shortness of breath. Gone were the general fatigue and the desire to throw fire at the park flowers until she was released from the task. To a fennec fox, running was the most natural thing in the world. It felt liberating, rejuvenating even. By the time she sped up the front walkway to Devon and Julian's home, she had hardly broken a sweat.

The door was unlocked, so she let herself inside. Most people would find it unfathomable not to use a deadbolt in the city, but the two homeowners in question weren't exactly 'most people.' Rae grinned to herself as she imagined how excited both of them would be if someone were ever to break in. Julian would call home and warn Devon ahead of time that it was happening, and Devon would lie in wait—silent as the grave, probably with popcorn. Together, they'd make the citizen's arrest of a lifetime, and most likely they wouldn't stop boasting about it for years to come.

She was still smiling away as she breezed through the living room and made a bee-line for Julian's closed door. The excitement of securing a partner-in-crime to finally help unlock her father's secrets was almost over-powering, and despite have borrowed Devon's heightened senses, she was so distracted she missed a couple of key indicators that something may be off.

The rustling of sheets. The sound of heavy breathing. An occasional moan.

She pushed open the door without a care in the world.

Then fled at the speed of light.

"I'M SORRY! OH MY GOODNESS I'M SO SORRY!"

She bolted down the hall, but not before the image was burned forever into her brain:

Julian and Angel...making the most of the morning.

A glass vase shattered against the wall behind her as she flew past. Switching into involuntary survival mode, Rae was surprised when Cassidy's tatù floated tentatively to the surface. Then she was severely tempted. Should she turn invisible? Literally just disappear from the face of the earth?

She was just mulling over the possibility when Julian emerged from the hall, clutching a sheet around his waist and looking like hell just warmed over.

They locked eyes and Rae turned a sickly shade of green, feeling as though his beloved girlfriend had just worked a freezing power on her.

"Jules, I'm so—"

"What the hell are you doing?" he cried. "Don't you knock?!"

"I'm so sorry!" she shrieked, still trying to scrub the image from her mind. "I know our plans were for a little later today, but I thought we could get an early—"

"WHERE IS SHE?!"

Rae shrank back against the front door as Angel's voice echoed down the hall.

"I'M GOING TO STRANGLE HER WITH HER STUPID PONYTAIL!"

Julian cast her an unsympathetic look, and she tried desperately to defend herself as the terrifying girl crashed around in the bedroom, getting dressed.

"Why didn't you see me coming in?" she countered, grasping at any and all straws she could think of. "This isn't just on me—"

"I was a little *busy*," Julian fired back, blushing to the tips of his ears.

Rae covered her eyes. "I remember." As if that wasn't bad enough, sheer panic took over and she heard herself saying, "On the bright side...your arms are looking super toned—"

"Get out of my house!"

She gulped and yanked open the front door, "Gladly."

"NOT SO FAST!"

Angel appeared suddenly before them, and the look on her face was worse than anything Rae could have imagined. There was finally a splash of color in her porcelain cheeks, but whether it was from being interrupted or that move Julian was doing earlier, Rae couldn't tell.

She tried to break the ice with a tentative smile of surrender. "Good morning, Angel. Hey, remember way back when I accidently walked in on you and Jules," she gulped, "...cuddling? Well, no harm, no foul right? I say, let's just let bygones be bygones—"

In times of trouble, she had a regrettable habit of speaking only in idioms.

A fork lodged itself in the wall right next to her head and she jumped back with a little yelp.

"Hey, hey," Julian quickly intervened, sensing that weaponizing the utensils was just the beginning of a slippery slope. "Honey," he took Angel cautiously by the hand, "why don't you take a nice shower and calm down? I'll deal with this one." He jerked his head to where Rae was bouncing nervously from foot to foot, muttering something about burying the hatchet.

Angel gave him a lethal look, before her face melted into the sweetest of smiles. Upon seeing it, Rae breathed a sigh of relief. But Julian's reaction was exactly the opposite. His entire body stiffened in alarm, freezing up to the point where it looked like he wasn't breathing.

"Uh...Jules?" Rae whispered anxiously.

It was then that she realized 'freezing' had been the operative word.

"Are you serious?" she said a little louder, her blatant disbelief giving her boldness in the face of fear. "You actually froze him?"

Angel turned that same dangerous smile onto her. "Well, I wasn't planning on it. In fact, I was *planning* on my morning turning out a lot differently. But thanks to a certain—"

"What's going on?"

Both girls whirled around as Devon wandered down the stairs, staring around the living room in wonder. Rae sucked in a quick breath. Really? Did she have to come over the second that he decided to take a shower? Did he have to walk downstairs without a shirt? *Did her cheeks have to blush like that?!*

Angel folded her arms across her chest, hardly sparing him a second glance. "Nothing. Go back upstairs," she snapped.

However, Devon was rarely one to do as he was told. He was already behind her when she made the command, and was examining Julian with a look of tired disapproval. "Angel—what did I tell you about freezing people in the house?"

Her hands twitched impatiently. "You said you'd consider it."

Devon's head snapped up and Rae bit back a smile. "No. I absolutely did *not* say I'd consider it. I said never, under any circumstances, was it to happen. Do you remember me saying that?"

Angel's chin jutted up and she sniffed. "Must have slipped my mind."

His blue eyes narrowed infinitesimally. "Let him go."

Incensed, Angel whipped her head around, sending her white blond hair spraying out in a wide arch behind her. "Look, Wardell, I'm kind of in the middle of something—"

"*Now*, Angela."

She made a rebellious sound, but flicked her fingers in the air. "Fine." There was a quiet gasp as Julian sprang back to life, but she didn't even bother turning around to see. "Now, as I was—"

"I didn't mean to see you naked!"

Rae cowered against the open door, already crippled by the anxiety of waiting for the other shoe to drop. The other three turned slowly towards her—their expressions ranging from amusement, to rage, to utter bewilderment.

"Alright...I definitely missed something," Devon murmured.

"Oh, come on," Angel snapped viciously, "like you didn't hear."

He pointed to a pair of earphones draped around his neck. "I didn't. I've had to start listening to deafening music anytime you and Jules start to..." His voice trailed off as his eyes flickered to Rae with sudden understanding. "...oh."

"Yeah," she muttered, her face turning red, "oh."

The corners of his lips twitched as he held back a smile. Then he cocked his head towards Angel before saying, "So she's about to kill you then, huh?"

Rae paled. "Not if she has even a single merciful bone in her body."

Angel's eyes narrowed. "Let's assume I don't."

Devon chuckled as he walked casually in between them. "It's always one thing or another with you, isn't it, Kerrigan?" He glanced back at her with a genuine smile, and for a moment the rest of the world seemed to fall away. For a moment, they were just themselves again—Devon and Rae. Inseparable. Not a care in the world. For a moment, everything was as it should be.

Then he remembered himself and stepped deliberately out of the line of fire.

"Well, good luck with that." He grabbed a shirt from a pile of clean laundry on the kitchen table and slipped it over his head. "Remember your training, and you'll do fine."

Julian ignored the joke and turned to him with a frown. "Where are you going?"

Only someone who had known Devon a long time could have detected the minute pause before he answered. "Debriefing for the Collins case. I'll only be a few hours."

The frown deepened, and Rae could have sworn she saw Julian's eyes flicker clairvoyant-white before darkening back to brown.

"Cool," he said easily. It was casual, but he didn't miss a single detail as he watched Devon pack a briefcase. "I'll see you later."

"Later." Devon slipped past Rae with a polite nod and disappeared down the steps.

She was far too hung up on the 'polite nod' to think of much of anything else, but Angel and Julian shared a quick look behind her back, staring after Devon's car as it raced down the drive.

It was quiet for a long time before Angel finally cleared her throat. "So why are you dressed like some kind of Nike assassin anyway?"

Rae looked down at her clothes in dismay. She'd thought she'd done a spectacular job. Then she remembered their cover and straightened up importantly.

"I've taken up jogging," she said with just a hair too much enthusiasm. "Julian has, too. We decided to go out at least once a day."

Angel didn't blink. "Jogging?"

Rae faltered a moment, but held her ground. "Yes, jogging."

Angel turned to Julian. "You hate jogging."

He shook his head innocently. "I love...jogging."

The word lived and died in the air between them. The more times they had said it, the more ridiculous it seemed to sound, and the more ridiculous Rae felt in her carefully crafted spandex.

Then, all at once, Julian sighed. "Fine. We're not really jogging."

Angel grinned. "You think?"

Rae tensed, but kept her eyes on Julian and trusted he would come through for her.

"The truth is I'm helping Rae with a project that's near and dear to her heart. Something personal." He took a breath and looked at his girlfriend intently. "It's something I promised to do."

A shiver ran up Rae's spine as she stared between them—both impressed by his quiet honesty, and worried as to whether or not it would work.

Angel's face didn't give much away. She simply stared back at him for a long moment before cocking her head to the side. "And I take it nobody else knows about this *personal* project?"

He shook his head, and she paused, absorbing it.

"And I take it you're not going to tell me what it is?"

There was a hint of curiosity in her voice, but he shut it down with a small smile. He shook his head again before stroking her hair back from her face. "Not my story to tell, love."

Please let this work. Please let this work.

"Okay, fine," she conceded suddenly. "You two can keep your little secret."

Rae's lips parted in surprise, but Julian just smiled knowingly.

There was more to his hot-tempered temptress than met the eye. But just as he turned on his heel to get dressed, she reached out and caught his arm with an impish smile. "Just keep in mind, Jules, every second that you're away, I'm going to be up in the bedroom planning a rematch. I only hope I don't get too bored waiting and decide to move on to something else..."

He hesitated for a second, completely thrown off course, before shaking his head with a grin. "That's cruel."

"Oh, just go," Rae interjected. "I don't want to spoil your fun twice in one day. Whatever it is we end up doing can wait until tomorrow. I'll just head home."

"Actually, Rae?" Angel's eyes were fixed on the open door. "One of the four horsemen of the apocalypse is here to see you."

One of the...what?

Rae closed her eyes as the cloying scent of self-importance and too much aftershave washed over her. She had a sinking idea of who that might be.

Turned out, she might be going to Guilder after all...

Chapter 5

"Mr. Mallins." Rae turned around with a sickly smile plastered to her face. "What an...unexpected surprise."

He stood wearing his usual eighteenth-century attire—complete with gloves and a driving cap—darkening the doorway like he owned the place.

"Miss Kerrigan," he smiled faintly as his eyes swept the room. "Keeping busy as usual, I see."

His gaze rested briefly on Angel still poised to kill, then Julian still clutching a towel around his bare waist, before landing on Rae. The tension in the room was undeniable, but it seemed to do nothing more than feed his efforts. He took his time, making them all twitch. "I decided to stop by because I heard a rumor you might be headed over to Guilder today."

Rae's heart skipped a beat. How the hell had he heard that? She'd only just decided to go last night. Had she told anyone besides...?

Her eyes flickered to Julian, but he frowned and shook his head a fraction of an inch. He hadn't told anyone.

She was about to ask Mallins himself, but the man interrupted—droning on in his dry monotone, "As fate would have it, I'm heading that way myself. I came to offer you a ride, as well as my company."

Rae truly didn't know which was worse. "How did you..." she tried again, but Mallins' lips turned up in a cracked smile. One look told her everything she needed to know. He wasn't going to say where he'd gotten his information. She might as well ask the kitchen sink. "Well, that's very," she cleared her throat, mind scrambling to come up with a plan, "that's very considerate of you."

Again her eyes flashed to Julian, but he was looking just as confused as she was. Confused, with a good deal of well-deserved agitation thrown in.

This was the President of the Privy Council they were talking about. Well, one of two acting presidents. Point was, there was no way in hell he just went around making house calls, offering ex-agents rides back to the school. There was something else going on here, and given the man in question they could only assume it was something rather sinister.

Julian stepped forward protectively. "Mr. Mallins, if you don't mind, I was also going to Guilder this morning. Perhaps I could join the two of you."

Rae slipped into Maria's telepathy. *Thanks, Jules.*

Except Mallins wasn't having it. He fixed Julian in his cold, emotionless stare, clearly sending shivers up everyone's spines. "I'm afraid that'll be impossible. Miss Kerrigan and I have things of a rather sensitive nature to discuss." His eyes travelled once more between Julian and Angel, before narrowing with a faint smirk. "Besides, it looks like you were in the middle of something."

Julian's handsome face flushed as his fingers tightened reflexively on the towel. He cast Rae another frustrated look and it appeared as though he might try to intervene again, but Mallins was looking at Angel now, and his attention was immediately diverted.

"I don't believe we've been introduced." Mallins inclined his head slightly, though he didn't extend his hand. "My name is Victor Mallins. And you are...?"

Rae had to give Angel credit—she was quick on her feet.

"Jaclyn Hunter. Nice to meet you."

Mallins smiled slowly, and Julian's knuckles turned white. "Miss Hunter." The smile widened. "The pleasure is all mine."

Another chill ran up Rae's spine. He knew who Angel was. There wasn't a doubt in her mind. But again—how? Did the PC have a list of Cromfield's people? Or a possible list of those he'd abducted? That wouldn't be too far-fetched. Lists of missing children were kept all the time in the real world; what's to say the PC didn't have a list? Surely Angel and Gabriel had been taken, not donated? What about Kraigan? Rae knew she was getting off topic, but how had Kraigan not been taken by Cromfield if her father knew about him?

She shook her head. *Focus, Rae. Mallins is just waiting for you to screw up.* They'd been incredibly careful. No one outside Carter, Beth, and their tiny group of friends had any idea as to Angel's real identity. And yet, somehow this man did.

Julian seemed to agree with Rae's thoughts, too, because he looked like he was having a mild heart attack.

Calm down, Rae instructed mentally. *Don't give him what he wants.*

Together, the three of them braced for whatever was going to come next—but it appeared that Victor was done with his little show.

Without so much as a glance behind, he turned and headed down the walkway to his car. "Grab your coat, Miss Kerrigan," he called over his shoulder. "I'll be waiting."

The door slammed shut, and the three of them turned to each other in panic.

"*That*?!" Rae demanded, turning to her psychic friend. "You didn't see *that* coming?!"

For the second time that morning, Julian gestured to his towel with frustration.

"I told you, I've been a little preoccupied."

"That's it." She shook her head disapprovingly. "No more sex for you."

Angel ignored them and took a step away from the door, shifting her weight nervously. "Was that who I think it was?"

"Victor Mallins," Rae confirmed, shaking her head at the prospect of a forty-minute car ride with him out of the city. She wouldn't put it at all past him to simply dump her body somewhere in the rolling English hills. "And yes. He's that charming all the time."

"How the hell did he even know you were here?" Julian murmured, scanning discreetly out the window. A dark town car sat idling impatiently by the side of the curb.

"I don't know," Rae answered, "but right now I think that's the least of our problems." She and Julian locked their eyes on Angel at the same time.

Angel glanced again outside but shook her head, physically calming down. After almost two decades of living in an underground cave with Jonathon Cromfield, it would take more than a morning visit with Victor Mallins to apparently rattle her now. "I'll be fine. I mean—he knows me, that's pretty obvious—but if he wanted to do something about it, it would have happened by now."

"What if that's not true?" Julian's voice dropped an octave as he stared at her fearfully. "What if he's just waiting for the right moment to make his move?" His face tightened painfully, and he slowly shook his head. "Angel, maybe we should think about—"

"No," she cut him off. "I'm not going into hiding again, so don't even mention it. I couldn't care less about the Privy Council. I'm staying right here with you."

"You might not care about the PC, but that doesn't mean that they've stopped caring about you," he insisted urgently. "If Mallins knows that you were Cromfield's lieutenant—that's treason right there. A man like him wouldn't just let something like that go. It doesn't matter if Carter personally pardoned you or not; it's a matter for the—"

"It's a matter for another time," Rae interrupted, glancing anxiously out the window as the car honked its horn. "I'll try to poke around and find out what Mallins knows, but in the meantime, just stay calm. Angel, keep your head down, and Jules...just stay with her, I guess. Now that you know who to keep an eye on, you'll be able to see if anything's coming."

She needn't have added this last part. Judging from the expression on his face, there was no way in heaven or hell Julian was letting Angel out of his sight.

"And what about you?" he asked quietly.

"Me?" Rae repeated, trying and failing to sound cheerful. "Looks like I just got a free ride to Guilder."

That 'free ride' to Guilder turned out to have certain strings attached. Forty minutes later, Rae was seriously considering jumping from the car and just running the rest of the way. She'd risk using Jennifer's or Devon's tatù just to get away from the man beside her.

"I hope it's not too cold for you," Victor said unsympathetically. "I prefer to keep the thermostat around forty-five. Keeps people sharp."

Rae forced her glare into a smile, and made a conscious effort to stop shivering. She was still in her little jogging outfit, and the thin material was doing nothing to shield her from the unforgiving air conditioning. "Not at all. I like it cold."

His lips turned up in a grin. "But of course. I'm sure you've picked up some temperature-regulating tatù over the years. I would imagine it would take quite a lot to get under your skin."

Quite a lot to get under my skin? What the hell is that supposed to mean?!

Chafing against his odd choice of words, Rae discreetly scooted as far away in her seat as possible and stared out the window, offering only a bland, "Mmm-hmm."

However, Mallins wasn't going to let her opt out of his little game so easily. He had carefully maneuvered it so that they would share a car ride—and he wasn't nearly finished yet. "So," he continued innocuously, "why is it that you were going to Guilder today?"

Her head snapped up to lock eyes with him for a moment before she leaned back against the leather seat with an air of innocence to match his own. "No particular reason. Just missed the campus. It's been a while. And I still have friends there."

"That's right." He pretended to be surprised; Rae had no problem detecting the mockery in his voice. "You were a mentor in your final year. I suppose there are still those at Guilder who feel a certain kinship to you."

Again with the cryptic passive aggression! Just say what you mean, creep!

He smoothed a non-existent wrinkle from his starched collar. "Rather strange, really."

Her eyes narrowed the slightest degree before she asked just as casually, "What is?"

"Just that you would be put in a position of authority over children still in their formative years. A *Kerrigan*," he answered with no pretense. "I suppose it was Carter who approved it."

Rae bristled, and for a moment she dropped her cool façade. "Yes, it was *President* Carter who suggested that I mentor. And yes, I did form a kinship with those kids. I'd like to think it was a good partnership for everyone involved. I got my community service hours to graduate, and they got hands-on help figuring out their new ink. Win-win."

Mallins' dark eyes zeroed in on her like a pair of black holes, sucking away all hope and chance of happiness. "Well it was certainly a win for you, wasn't it, Miss Kerrigan? All those new abilities. I suppose you'd leap at an opportunity such as that."

A wave of bile rose up in her throat, but she swallowed it down. "I don't know exactly what you're insinuating—"

But just then, a security guard tapped on the glass and Rae jumped in her seat. She hadn't realized how far they'd gotten. They were now stopped at the gates of Guilder.

"Morning, Mr. Mallins," the guard said routinely. "Just one guest with you today?"

The first thing Rae noticed about the man was the heavy firearm strapped in a holster at his hip. The standard PC taser was not far behind. The second thing was the fact that the guard was there at all. She didn't remember there being active security at the gates when she was going to Guilder. Her eyes drifted past him to an official check-point bunker right behind. When had this stuff gotten here? It looked like the school was gearing up for battle or some kind of siege.

"Yes, Ethan, just the one guest." Mallins turned to Rae with those same expressionless eyes as they were waved forward. "The very thing that brings me to the reason I brought you here today, Miss Kerrigan."

"Yeah," she shifted nervously as the familiar scenery flew by, "what's that?"

"To find out if you are indeed still a guest, or if you've decided to accept the Privy Council's offer of employment. I'm sure this will come as no shock to you, but we aren't exactly accustomed to waiting for a reply..."

Are you a guest, or are you an agent?

Question of the day. And he wanted a split-second reply.

Rae stared at him for a second, mind racing, before all of a sudden it hit her. The solution to all her immediate problems. The 'in' that she and Julian had been looking for.

She wanted to research the workings of the Privy Council? She wanted to troll around in their databases, searching for the answers she was aching to know?

Well, what better way to get inside than by open invitation?

A glowing smile stretched across her face, as she stared back evenly across the car. "I'm afraid you're not going to like my answer..."

A muscle in Mallins' temple twitched with frustration, but other than that he remained in a state of perfect calm. "You've decided to accept, then?"

"I've decided to accept."

It was so simple, she was surprised it hadn't occurred to her earlier.

"To be an agent once more?"

"Yes, to be an agent." She was finding it nearly impossible to stifle her grin. The more times she reiterated her decision, the redder Mallins' face seemed to become.

Yet when he spoke, his voice was as dry and cracked and unreadable as ever. "I suspected as much. In fact, it's the reason I offered you a ride. It gave me the chance to kill two birds with one stone."

Rae had never particularly liked that phrase, and it seemed particularly ominous coming from Mallins' mouth now. "What's that supposed to mean?"

He glanced at her blandly as their driver pulled into a parking spot near the Oratory. "Well, as an agent of the Privy Council, you'll be reporting directly to me." He paused long enough to let the chilling ramifications of that statement sink in before continuing. "And I've never been one to waste time. Now that you're officially employed once more by the PC, I brought you here to brief you on your first mission."

Rae blinked. Her first mission? She'd just signed on again—what—two seconds ago? And he already had her first mission in mind?

She had been hoping to get a little time at Guilder, enough time to formulate a plan. She and Julian would still probably have enough friends and access to get into the main computer system, and a general search was all she'd really need. Just two simple names... and all the mysterious, incriminating information that came along with them.

"You already have a mission picked out?" she couldn't help but ask, stalling as she was struck by a sudden wave of nerves as to what it might be. By the way he was looking at her now, she wouldn't be surprised if it had some serious kamikaze overtones.

"Oh yes. As I said, I anticipated your eventual re-employment."

"You certainly did," Rae muttered, following as he slipped out of the car and stepped out into the bright summer sun. "You also happened to know that I was planning on heading over here today, and that I'd be at Julian and Devon's new house." She let it hang between them, but he didn't reply. But she matched his pace as he headed into the Oratory, refusing to let him off the hook. "How is that exactly, sir? Or do I need to touch you to find out?" she pressured.

There was a raspy, wheezing sound that took her a minute to identify as a chuckle.

"Oh, Miss Kerrigan, what kind of President would I be if I didn't keep a close eye on all of my assets?" He stopped so suddenly she almost ran into him. "And you are one of my assets now, are you not?"

The Oratory door shut loudly behind her, and she jumped in her skin.

"All of you are," he continued softly. "You, Devon Wardell, Julian, and Molly. Your whole merry little band. You all work for me now."

Rae jutted up her chin, unable to keep the blatant defiance from her face. "I don't know about Julian and Molly. They're still thinking it over."

Again, Mallins chuckled. "Why, Miss Kerrigan, I'm afraid you're behind the times. Both Mr. Decker and Miss Skye have already been officially reinstated. Mr. Decker was just this very morning."

Rae resisted the urge to roll her eyes, thoroughly unimpressed. Of course Julian signed up this morning. He had probably seen her signing up this afternoon, had guessed what she was up to, and made a quick phone call to follow suit.

Molly was a different story. Why the hell hadn't she mentioned she had signed back up with the PC? It wasn't exactly the kind of thing you kept to yourself.

The last time they'd talked about it, her best friend had seemed almost as reluctant as her. In fact, the only one who had been excited about the PC's offer had been Devon. None of the rest of them were as easy to convince and so quick to believe once again in the system. After all, why should they be? That very system had failed them and the hybrids they were trying to save, in more ways than Rae could imagine.

"Well, I'm happy to hear it," she said, disconcerted but hiding it well. "Now that we're all on the same team again, maybe we can put this whole summer behind us and get started on something new."

Again, Mallins' face twisted up into a rather frightening smile—wrinkled with age and malice. "I couldn't agree more. In fact," he slipped through a side doorway and led her down a darkened hall to a waiting room, "I was hoping to introduce you to your new partner."

He pulled open the door and the tall man waiting in the corner turned around.

"Or should I say, your *old* partner."

Chapter 6

Rae spoke without thinking, her surprise getting the better of her. "Devon?"

He stood, just as shocked as she was, looking like he, too, had been similarly yanked from his morning plans and ushered here instead. "What're you doing here?" he asked curiously. "I thought I was meeting my—"

"I thought you were debriefing the Collins case," Rae interrupted, echoing his words to Julian just an hour before.

"No," it was Victor who answered, as he paced behind his desk, "Mr. Wardell was in the library. Somewhere you could stand to go more often, Miss Kerrigan. Our minds need training just like our bodies if we want to keep them sharp."

Devon rolled his eyes and flashed her a small smile behind Mallins' back.

Rae stared, unsure and troubled. Not about Mallins, but about Devon. What was so embarrassing about the library? Why would he feel the need to cover it up?

Julian knew he was lying... She put it together in her next breath. *This isn't the first time this has happened. Julian already knew he wasn't telling the truth.* Her blue eyes narrowed slightly as she stared back into his. She was surprised once again to see that he was looking at her with a similar distrust.

Probably wondering why the hell I'm here at Guilder with Mallins when I repeatedly said it was the last place on earth I wanted to be. My surprise trip to NYC probably didn't help either.

"You finish jogging already?" he asked softly, gesturing down to her athletic clothes.

Her skin flushed light pink, but she stared back evenly. "About as quickly as you finished up with the Collins case. In the *library*."

"That's neither here nor there," Mallins interrupted, willfully oblivious to the tension emanating between the two teenagers. "I brought you two here to brief you on your next mission."

There was a brief pause and then—

"Wait—*what*?!" Rae exclaimed, looking at Devon like she'd never seen him before. "*Devon's* going to be my new partner?"

Devon looked just as distressed as her, turning in supplication to Mallins. "Sir, after everything that's happened, I really think that we should probably be paired with different—"

"Excuse me?!" Rae cut him off, mid-complaint, stunned to hear that he was trying to get rid of her, blatantly ignoring the fact that she was trying to do the same. "Oh, I'm sorry, Dev, I didn't realize I was no longer up to your standards."

His eyes flicked momentarily to Mallins before he turned back to her, forgetting himself as well. "That's not what this is about, and you know it. Do you really think that you and I are in the best position right now to work as partners? I can't think of anything worse."

"Than working with me?" Rae put her hands on her hips with a dark scowl. "You can't think of anything worse than working with me?"

"Oh come on! Like you want to work with me?"

"Actually, I absolutely don't," she hissed, "but that's not the same thing!"

He threw up his hands. "How's it not the same thing?!"

A throat cleared loudly between them, and they both turned to see Mallins watching them with a bland smile. "Then it's a good thing it isn't up to either of you, isn't it?"

"Sir," Devon tried again, lowering his voice beseechingly, "there has to be someone else you can pair us with. I could go back with Julian, and Rae could start working with Molly—"

"Mr. Wardell, I made these assignments myself. Let me assure you, they are final." He glared at Devon over the top of his spectacles. "Furthermore, I have to say that I'm surprised at your behavior. Not only do you and Miss Kerrigan already have a working relationship to fall back on, but I was told to expect more from you. This level of insubordination is beneath you."

If he'd slapped Devon, it couldn't have stung more.

His tan skin turned a particular shade of crimson before he fell back a step, bowing his head respectfully. "Yes, sir. I apologize."

Rae was not so easy to appease. "So this *special* mission you thought of for just the two of us..." she crossed her arms over her chest. "What is it?"

Behind Mallins' back, Devon fought back a scowl. He'd always cautioned her on showing the proper deference to authority figures, and was always appalled when she blew it off. Truth be told, she said it half to bait him. But he ignored her— keeping his eyes firmly on the wall.

Mallins reached into his desk and pulled out two manila folders, handing one to each of them. "It's basic reconnaissance. Should be simple enough even for the two of you."

Devon flinched and started thumbing through, but Rae kept hers closed, staring unblinkingly back at Mallins. "And who are we doing recon of?"

"His name is Jackman White. Son of an oil tycoon and heir to a small fortune. He's here in London for a business conference before flying off to Milan on Friday."

Devon frowned, speed-reading with his tatù. "And what is the Council's interest in him?"

Mallins' colorless eyes narrowed. "We think he may also be in contact with the Xavier Knights. You'll be tasked with searching his office at the hotel. We need to know what, if any, information has been passed between them."

Again, Rae slipped into Maria's telepathy.

Or we could just ask Luke.

Devon's shoulders tightened and he flashed her a look that said one thing and one thing only: 'Stay out of my head.'

She rolled her eyes and tried again. *What? First you don't want to be partnered with me, and now we're not even speaking? What's next? You're going to start deleting pictures of me in your phone?*

A muscle in his jaw twitched and he shifted impatiently from foot to foot, unable to answer back but clearly dying to give her a piece of his mind.

On the other side of the room Mallins was pacing back and forth, saying something about the importance of this work to the Privy Council. Except, Rae and Devon were in their own little world.

It isn't enough that you lied to Julian this morning about where you were going—now you're going to stand there and try to shut me out as well?

His blue eyes narrowed into a smoldering glare and he looked her pointedly up and down, making careful note of her spandex clothes.

That doesn't mean anything. Maybe I actually did go jogging— you don't know. I'm not the one who's going around actively lying about their whereabouts.

His lips thinned into a hard line and he cocked an eyebrow sarcastically.

Don't give me that! I already told you why I went to New York. It was to visit my aunt and uncle.

He shook his head a fraction of an inch.

Argh! You can be so childish sometimes—

"Mr. Wardell," Mallins' voice interrupted their silent back and forth. "Are you even listening to me?"

Yeah, Devon...

They were dismissed about half an hour later, having been thoroughly briefed with strict instructions to pack a pair of bags and check in to the same London hotel where Jackman White would be staying.

What the hell kind of name is 'Jackman White' anyway? Rae thought as they stepped out of the Oratory into the bright summer sunlight. *What mind of a mother looks down at their newborn and thinks, 'I know, I'm going to name you Jackman.' Must be an heiress thing...*

A sharp tug on her sleeve jerked Rae out of her trance, and she looked up to see Devon standing in front of her, arms crossed over his chest, a giant scowl on his face. "I want to thank you for that in there. Really. I love being the victim of your one-sided telepathy."

She glared up at him. "Can't blame a girl for being curious."

"No, but I can blame a girl for being ridiculous in the middle of a mission brief with the President of the Privy Council."

"One of *two* presidents, Devon. I know you and Mallins are all, 'Go PC!' but in case you forgot Carter is the president as well."

Devon's handsome face grew cold. "That's not the way it is and you know it. You know exactly how I feel about both Carter and Mallins. There's no comparison."

"But you're certainly a fan of the Council again." She folded her arms across her chest and stood up as tall as she could to face him. "I don't think you wasted more than twenty-four hours before you signed back up with them."

He threw up his hands in exasperation. "What would you have had me do, Rae? You signed up with them, too!"

"Yeah, but that's different!"

"*How* is it different?!"

"It just—" She caught herself and brought her fingers up to her temples. It was different because she was doing it simply to infiltrate the society and get the information she needed. But it's not like she could very well tell Devon that, now could she? Not when she and Julian had both sworn to leave him and Molly out of it to protect them. "It just is," she finished rather lamely.

He eyed her defeated posture, and his face softened as he took a step back. "Look," he began, raking his fingers back through his hair, "if we're going to do this, we're going to have to find a way to work together. This is an official mission. We can't be like...like this."

"I know," she sighed. She was being ridiculous. "I'm sorry for earlier. For talking in your head. I just..." Her voice trailed off as she finally lifted her eyes to look at him. "Devon, I don't know how to do this."

The flash of honesty surprised them both, and for a moment there were no walls between them. He looked down at her with pained understanding, then he bowed his head.

"I know," he muttered, his dark hair spilling down his forehead. "I don't either."

They were quiet a long while, standing in silence in the tall grass as the birds and the breeze struck up a peaceful descant around them.

"How can we just be friends?" she whispered, not daring to look at him. "When I see you, I don't see a friend. I see something so much more. If we can't be that...I don't know what we are."

"Rae..." he spoke so softly it was almost hard for her to hear, "you know why we're doing this. You and me? Us? That's forever to me. And that's not something we can rush into. You..." he swallowed hard, but pushed himself forward, "you kissed Gabriel. You're not—*we're* not in the same place about this."

"We are." She looked up, staring into his clear eyes. "I promise we are."

But she also remembered her promise to herself. Devon was right. She'd kissed Gabriel. That didn't come without repercussions. He might be claiming this time gap was for her, but he needed some time to work things out for himself. And on that note, she needed time herself as well. Time to find out the answer to her father's riddle. Time when Devon wasn't around to get hurt.

"You're right," she continued suddenly, dropping her gaze. "It's probably best that we just take it easy for a while. Let things cool off."

His eyes tightened painfully, but he nodded. "Cool off. Right."

Every part of her ached to reach out and take his hand. From the look on his face, she was willing to bet he was feeling the same way. But it was like there was a wall between them. One that had sprung up overnight. One that neither one of them knew how to cross.

And no matter the reasons, no matter the rationalizations and benefits to both sides, Rae had a sinking feeling that if they weren't careful that wall might just crush them both.

"So what do we do about this?" She waved the manila folder in the air between them, trying to move the conversation along.

It was the right thing to say. Devon had been trained to be the perfect soldier. The second she circled the discussion back around to work, he snapped back to attention.

"We do our jobs," he said briskly. "We'll go back to London, pack, and check into the hotel at four. With any luck, we can break into White's room tonight and have the whole thing wrapped up by tomorrow morning."

She nodded and forced a quick smile. "Sounds good."

"Okay then."

"Okay."

"So...bye."

"Yeah, bye."

Their eyes met, and they actually laughed nervously at their own awkwardness. Then, before things could get any worse, Devon turned on his heel and headed back towards the parking lot. He was halfway there before he turned back and called, "I forgot that you came with Mallins." He sounded a bit uncertain. "Do you...do you need a ride?"

Rae hesitated. She hadn't even thought about it, but the truth was she *did* need a ride. Then again, she literally couldn't imagine a forty-minute car ride with Devon right now. They'd had enough trouble simply trying to say goodbye. A long drive through the countryside? Probably best to leave until later...

"Uh—I'm good actually. But thanks. I'll see you at four."

"Cool."

He turned on his heel and disappeared over the ridge in the trail. Meanwhile, Rae glanced discreetly around the campus before darting beneath a towering willow. Once she was confident that no one could possibly see, she stripped off her fake jogging clothes and left them in a spandex pile in the tall grass. A moment later, she slipped into her prized eagle tatù and took to the sky, leaving the wretched morning far behind her.

Despite being somewhat impractical, Rae had to admit that Rob's eagle ink was one of her all-time favorites. There was something about feeling the lift of the wind beneath your wings that had absolutely no earthly comparison. That being said, it did come with one huge drawback.

The landing.

Rae circled around her penthouse three times, peering into all the windows in all the rooms before she was finally satisfied that it was deserted. Once she was, she crammed her football-sized body through a partially-open window and soared into the living room. It was rather odd, seeing everything from this perspective. She perched on a picture frame, cocked her head, and looked around for a moment. Then her sharp eyes landed on the clock hanging on the wall.

Already coming up on noon. When did that happen?

It's so hard to keep track of these things as a bird...
She hopped down onto a Persian rug and shifted back, feeling her bones elongate and stretch as her blanket of feathers was replaced with tumbling raven-colored curls and a layer of glowing, porcelain skin.

There. Everything back to normal. Right on schedule.
She was just getting back to her feet when the front door burst open.

Then everything started going very suddenly wrong.

For a second both of them just stood there.

She and Gabriel.

His eyes swept over her naked body as his lips parted in shock. All the color drained from her face as she simultaneously wished she was dead, and prayed she no longer had any feathers.

Then they sprang into action.

She snatched a fur blanket off the sofa to cover herself, while he collapsed against the kitchen counter throwing back his head with clear, unadulterated laughter.

At first she couldn't help but be thrilled. This was the old Gabriel. Careless, effervescent, and radiating pure energy. The sight of it warmed her heart. To be honest, a part of her hadn't thought she'd ever hear the sound of that laugh again.

Then she remembered *why* he was laughing and her skin darkened to an angry shade of red.

"Yeah, yeah, very funny," she growled, shifting impatiently in her blanket. "You know, I'd forgotten how completely insufferable you are."

Unfortunately, that only made him laugh harder. He doubled over against the counter, completely unable to speak as little tears slipped down his cheeks.

"What?!" she demanded. "You try transforming into a bird."

His fingers came up over his face as he gasped for breath. "Oh, thank the Maker! You transformed into a bird. That makes so much more sense." Then he lost it all over again.

"Why else did you think I was surrounded by a circle of feathers?"

"I wasn't going to ask about the feathers." She cast him a dubious look, and he held up his hands. "Hey, we all have our quirks."

An involuntary giggle slipped through her lips, and she smiled at him resentfully. "You are the absolute worst. And you have the absolute worst timing in the whole world."

"Quite the contrary," he chuckled. "It looks like I got here not a moment too soon. I only wish I could have seen you...well...molting."

There was a beat of silence, then they both burst out laughing.

It was laughter they hadn't done together in a long while. Completely uninhibited and relaxed, but at the same time spirited and gasping for air. It went on for a long time, and even when it died down their smiles lingered long after.

"I've missed you," Rae found herself saying, smiling at him from across the room.

He picked himself off the counter, and crossed the floor— looking years younger than he had before. "Yeah." His dimples flashed as he shot her a grin. "I missed you, too." His hand reached out, and he extracted a long eagle feather that had tangled in her hair.

"Friends?" she asked hopefully. The feathers had been there when she first shifted; as she'd learned to be more graceful with the ability, it had become a kind of addition.

His eyes sparkled and shook his head with a grin. "Oh no— you know friends has never been good enough for me."

Her mouth fell open in amazement, but while he didn't seem to be joking, he wasn't in the least bit upset with her either. He simply stood there, his fingers twisting around a stray curl, as his eyes danced with that old, mischievous smile.

"Gabriel..." Although she didn't want to spoil the happy mood, she felt as though she needed to be clear. "There's still no...I mean...I still want Devon."

He shrugged, looking completely unbothered by the information. "Well, then it looks like we're back exactly where we started."

His undaunted enthusiasm was catching, and she felt herself grinning along before she realized what was happening. "Oh yeah? And where's that?"

He shook his head with a mock sigh. "You're still pining for the lesser man, and I'm still here. Gorgeous, unattached, and miraculously unfazed by the fact that you just turned into a bird."

Another giggle burst through her lips, and she pulled the fur tighter around herself, hiding her blushing face in its folds. "I can't believe that just happened..."

"You better believe it. It's a sight I'll remember forever." He tapped his temple with a wide grin. "Photographic memory."

"Well, isn't that just perfect?" she said sarcastically, shaking her head in amusement at the look of sheer victory plastered all over his face.

Yet the longer she looked, the more she found herself growing nervous. She really had missed this—more than she realized. Their playful back and forth. Their carefree banter. But most of all she had missed the sincerity behind it. Gabriel was one of the few people in the world who would always call it exactly how it was, no matter how potentially upsetting it might be. And while his feelings for her might be potentially hazardous to their health, at least they were all out in the open. All cards on the table.

She was anxious because...she didn't want to lose all that.

"Hey," he said suddenly, his face growing serious as he stared at her, "what's wrong?"

"Nothing, I just..." An unexpected wave of emotion crashed through her whole body, and she bit her lip to keep back the tears. "I really missed this."

His face softened tenderly, and without seeming to think about it he reached out and pulled her into a warm embrace. She sighed as she buried her head in his chest. Her shoulders relaxed, and for the first time in what seemed like forever she felt as though she'd gotten at least one thing back on track. At least one part of her crazy, upside-down life had finally fallen back into alignment.

Then his hand drifted a little lower, and she slapped it away with a grin.

Yep—everything was exactly how they'd left it.

Chapter 7

What exactly does one wear to a swanky London hotel on a fake date/super spy mission with the newly platonic love of their life?

These were the kinds of questions Rae normally asked Molly. If this was a normal situation. And apparently her best friend had taken this time—in Rae's time of need—to become one of those obnoxiously happy couples who was never around. Rae was on her own.

She flipped frantically through a couple of fashion magazines she had found stashed under Molly's bed, casting nervous glances all the while at the clock. Four p.m. was getting closer and closer, but she was still no closer to being packed than when she and Devon had parted ways this morning at Guilder.

To be fair, most of the time crunch was her fault. After she had finally extracted herself long enough to put on clothes, she and Gabriel had spent the afternoon together. Laughing, talking, eating—generally just wasting time in good company. She had no idea how good it would feel to just put aside all her heavy hidden agendas for a moment and act like a normal eighteen-year-old. The relaxation was addictive, and, frankly, she couldn't imagine a better person to do it with than Gabriel.

It made her feel guilty. She should be doing it with Devon. However, that wasn't possible at the moment. Gabriel knew how to make the complicated things in life... well, easy.

Aside from his occasional advances—all of which were so ludicrously over the top they could hardly be considered serious—Gabriel was the perfect companion. He was honest, funny, engaging, and entirely too bold. It was a lethal combination, and one to which she could see herself losing many afternoons if she wasn't careful. If she had been worried that this newfound forgiveness of his was a passing phase, those fears were soon laid to rest. According to him, the only thing that had changed between them was that now he had seen her naked. This was a point he continually circled back to until she finally threw him out at three-thirty to get ready.

She wished she had his courage, his ability to move forehead, his cockiness. He'd be an amazing agent for the PC. A real agent, though she had hesitated in telling him that.

Puffing out a hot breath, she forced herself to focus. As of this moment, she was strapped for time. The empty suitcase on her bed bore guilty witness to her procrastination. The second hand of the clock echoed in her ears.

She was still fretting over exactly what to bring when there was a knock on the door.

Her head whipped up in alarm. There was still twenty more minutes! Was Devon that early? Was she that screwed?!

"Just a..." she raced around, pulling a bathrobe over her pajamas, "just a minute!"

There was a metallic grinding in the lock, and the front door pushed open of its own accord. Soft footsteps padded across the kitchen to her bedroom as she blurred back and forth between her empty bag and her closet, tossing random armfuls of stuff inside.

"Nice packing."

She skidded to a halt and chuckled with relief. Julian, not Devon.

He was leaning up against her doorframe, eyeing her pathetic attempts with amusement. "Do you really think you're going to need a parka over at the Savoy? They must have changed the dress code since I left..."

"Wait! You've been there?!" She whirled around with wide eyes and gestured helplessly to her suitcase. "Jules, you've got to help me! I'm completely out of my element here!"

"First tell me why you even have a parka."

She tossed a pillow at his head. "I'm serious! I know it's this super luxurious hotel, but it's not like we're actually going to be 'hotel-ing.' We're there for reconnaissance."

Julian plopped down onto the bed with a grin. "So what's the problem?"

"What the heck am I supposed to wear? Do I bring a jumpsuit or a ball gown?"

"*Well*," he began importantly, stretching out on the mattress and picking up one of her magazines, "I always bring both. Although I often find that my jumpsuit clashes with my gown."

"You are just *so* helpful," she murmured, removing the parka and turning back to her closet with a hopeless sigh. "Remind me to be just as helpful the next time you have a problem..."

He ignored her and cocked his head to the side, frowning slightly at the lethal-looking corsets on some of the models. "You found these under Molly's bed?" he asked with a smile.

Rae nodded, looking tired. "That's right. The way some people stash chocolates and porn under the mattress, our little Molly stashes Vogue."

He snorted. "Well, that was predictable."

"Not as predictable as you *not* helping me with my imminent deadline."

"Just pack clothes, Rae. Nice clothes," he said, completely disinterested. This time, he turned the magazine halfway upside-down, struggling to understand the mechanics of Italian lacing. "I don't get it...how are you supposed to breathe?"

Rae glanced over as she conjured a pair of stilettos into her bag. "You're not. Fashion is pain, my friend."

He picked up one of the shoes with a raised eyebrow. "I'll say. I think I could actually kill someone with this, you know."

She shot him a hard look. "Don't think the thought hasn't crossed my mind..."

He chuckled and tossed it back on the bed. "I said nice clothes, didn't I? What else do you want from me?"

She sighed and tossed some black leather tights on top of the stilettos. "Sorry. I'm just...I have a feeling this is not going to be one of my favorite missions."

His face softened sympathetically. "Yeah, I saw. Sorry I couldn't give you guys a head's up. I saw it happening just a minute before it actually did. Otherwise I would have texted."

"That's okay. No one could have stopped it one way or another."

He shook his head with a small frown. "I just don't get it. After everything that's happened, why would Mallins want to pair you and Devon together? Or him and me? Or even you and me? We're probably the four most controversial agents the PC has had since your mom and Jennifer. Why wouldn't they want to space us out with older, more reliable people?"

Rae paused in surprise, her hands frozen around a hanger. She had never thought about it like that, but it was absolutely true. Aside from the controversy with her parents, the Council had never before experienced such blatant opposition from their own agents.

"Maybe it's just damage-control," she guessed. "They want to contain the spread of our impertinence. It's like a virus."

Julian cocked an eyebrow. "A virus?"

Rae grinned. "Maybe they're worried we'll unionize."

They laughed for a while, and eventually lapsed back into silence. Julian stretched out and read the magazine, Rae conjuring random pieces of clothes and tossing them into her bag.

After a couple minutes, her eyes flashed up to him tentatively. This was a subject she didn't want to breach, especially with Julian, but something he had said earlier kept looping back in her mind.

"Jules?" she asked quietly.

He glanced her way. "Yeah?"

"What did you mean...he's not happy."

Their eyes met for a long moment.

Then Julian looked down with a sigh. "Of course he's not happy, Rae. He's in love with you. And you're not together. How the hell could he be happy?"

Her eyes dropped to her half-packed bag. "I thought I should...I thought it was best that I give him some space. I know he needs it...you should have seen him at the meeting today. And then of course, it would keep him out of harm's way while you and I look into my dad's letter."

Julian gazed at her intently, before nodding slowly. "Yeah, that's the plan."

For whatever reason, her eyes began to water and she looked quickly away, masking it under the guise of conjuring herself a black camisole. "Well, anyways...I guess it's for the best, so I should just put it out of my head—"

Julian's dark eyes softened with pity. "Rae?"

A few tears spilled over, and she wiped them quickly off her cheeks. "Yeah?" She turned to him with a forced a smile—a smile that wouldn't fool anyone.

He opened his mouth to say something, and knowing Julian it would have been something good. But much to her surprise, he didn't say a word. He simply stared at her, peering gently into her eyes. Then he glanced down at the magazine in his lap, and his face lit up with a secret smile. "Wear that one."

Rae glanced down in surprise at the dress he was pointing at. "That one?"

His eyes twinkled.

"That one."

By the time four o'clock rolled around, Rae was dressed, packed, and ready for anything the night decided to throw at her. She stood fidgeting out on the curb, nervously smoothing down her long trench coat as her other hand fiddled with the handle on her bag. Ignoring Julian's advice, she'd decided to wait down by the road instead of making Devon come up to the apartment. They'd already run into each other twice by accident today; both times were like pulling teeth. Best to keep things as professional as possible. At least as far as the mission was concerned.

Her hand tightened around the leather strap as a sports car came flying from around the corner and screeched to a stop in front of the curb. Rae stifled a smile. Devon may act with the wisdom and responsibility of one far beyond his years, been when it came to cars he was just like every other nineteen-year-old guy.

He hopped out onto the sidewalk, grinning from ear to ear from the rush of speed and adrenaline. He was so distracted he almost ran into her standing in front of the door. "Oh crap! Sorry! I didn't see you." He caught himself quickly, lowering his hands as they reached out automatically to steady her. "Why are you down here?"

When he said it out loud, it suddenly seemed rather stupid.

"Oh, you know," she diverted, picking up her bag and carrying it over to the car, "just trying to get a move on things. We don't want to be late or—"

"I'll get that." His fingers slipped through hers and eased the suitcase out of her hand. When she looked up, he gave her a quirky smile. "We *are* dating, after all."

She froze in place, eyebrows disappearing into her hair. "Uh...excuse me?"

He realized his mistake at once, and turned a thousand shades of red as he hurried to fix it. "For the mission, I mean. We're dating for the mission. That's our cover." He set her suitcase in the backseat next to his, blushing all the while, his adorable dimple showing as he avoided her gaze. "It's how we're supposed to get close enough to White to put a bug on him. There's some big charity event this evening at the hotel. We'll tag him there, and then duck out early to break into his office."

Rae nodded swiftly, trying to act nonchalant. "Sounds good. With any luck, we won't even have to stay overnight. We can just leave the second we're done in his office."

Why...the hell did I just say that?

The second the words were out of her mouth, she regretted them. She hadn't intended them to come out so harsh. She was just having trouble finding her footing here. Fake relationships were hard enough—and then to attempt one with your brand new ex? Was there a rule book here or something? Maybe she could read it, and then use it to hit herself over the head...

Devon flashed her a quick look and she hurried to correct herself.

"I just meant it's a good plan. We should be in and out with no trouble."

"Yeah, sure." He pulled open her door, gesturing her inside. "No trouble."

"Dev, I really didn't mean anything by—"

"Listen, Rae... hang on." He shut the door before she could slide inside, and turned around to face her. "We need to figure this out. Right here, right now. This isn't us going back and forth at your apartment tonight; it's a Privy Council-sanctioned mission." His fingers raked nervously through his hair. "And not to put too fine a point on it, but after what we've put the Council through these last couple of months, we need to hit a home run here."

Rae paused on *what we've put the Council through* for a moment, but let it go. He was right. This wasn't the time for bickering or unsteady ground. They needed to be certain. As had become their surreal daily reality, lives were at stake. "You're absolutely right," she said quietly. "So what do we do?"

Their eyes met for a moment, and it looked like he was thinking things over hard. Then he straightened up suddenly, and cleared his throat. "You forget about your past with me, and I forget about my past with you. For twenty-four hours, we have a clean slate. No baggage. No tension. No history. We're just two agents posing as a couple on a mission. We keep things professional."

It sounded fine in theory. But in practice...? They'd have to wait and see.

But however unrealistic his plan might be, Rae latched onto it like a life-raft. In a lot of ways it was exactly what she needed to hear. No strings. No awkward half-sentences. No constantly putting her foot in her mouth and then blushing to high heaven.

Their relationship might be as convoluted and warped as they came, but if he wanted her to treat him like an agent? That was something she knew how to do.

"Keep things professional," she repeated with a slightly relieved smile. "I can do that." Without another thought she slipped off her long trench coat and climbed into the car, beating him to close the door as she settled her things around her. The clock on the dash read just a little after four. They would make it to the hotel and be ready for the event tonight with time to spare. She was just giving her lip gloss a cursory check in the mirror when she realized that Devon was still standing right outside the window where she'd left him—staring at her through the glass. A faint chill ran up her arms as she remembered she was wearing only a simple tube top with some dark fitted jeans. It hadn't seemed to matter much under the coat.

He blinked quickly and averted his gaze, circling around behind the car to get to the driver's seat. But as he crossed behind the rear window she could have sworn she saw a hint of a grin.

"You might be able to keep things professional," he breathed to himself—so soft that even with his tatù, it was almost impossible to hear. "Now I hope to hell I can. Damn!"

The Savoy was everything Rae had imagined and much more. From the second they pulled up and a valet took their keys, to the moment they were escorted to their suite on the top floor, she couldn't help but shake the feeling that somewhere driving along to road to get here she must have transformed into royalty.

This must be how Sarah feels all the time, she thought as a second attendant reached for her bag with a pair of white velvet gloves. She had decided to put her trench coat back on; tube tops and the Savoy didn't really fit in the same sentence, but she surrendered her other things with a gracious smile. *I could get used to it. Maybe Devon and I could go under cover later at the palace...?*

"Yo—Grace Kelly. You still with me?"

Rae looked up in surprise to see that the attendants had left, and she and Devon were alone in the room.

He was standing beside their pile of luggage, looking at her with an amused grin. "You want to go back to the palace again, don't you?"

She narrowed her eyes and shot him a superior scowl. "Using your weird talent of guessing my thoughts isn't exactly keeping things professional. A normal agent wouldn't know me that well."

"Oh, I beg to differ," he countered, sauntering towards her across the gilded floor. "An agent has to know their partner like the back of their own hand. You wouldn't believe half the stuff Julian and I have learned about each other over the years."

They both paused and she cocked her head questioningly to the side.

"Okay," Devon flushed self-consciously, "that came out weirder than I meant."

Rae giggled and rotated in a slow circle to take in the general splendor. The ceilings were high and lined with crown molding, the carpets were that plush, sink-your-toes-into-it decadence that her aunt always wanted but they never could afford, and all the furniture was designer. In fact, the one thing that kept running through her mind as she looked around was that this place was exactly the kind of design aesthetic that Molly had been aiming for but that Rae kept ruining with her eclectic taste and Moroccan bath mats.

Devon cleared his throat loudly behind her. "In the effort of further keeping things professional, I will refrain from mentioning that you're probably thinking about how much Molly would love this right now."

Rae bit her lip and turned back to him with a smile. "Yeah, that would probably be best."

"I also won't say that this reminds me, really strongly, of Heath Hall."

Rae's heart skipped a beat. Heath Hall was the place where she and Devon had gotten back together. The place where he had professed his love; first to her and then to the President of the Privy Council, choosing their relationship over his career once and for all. It was also the first place that they...well, it was a lot of firsts.

"Yeah," her voice got quieter and she dropped her eyes, "you probably shouldn't say that either."

Looking a little guilty for breaking his own rules, he cleared his throat again and gestured to the different doorways leading off from the living room. "Kitchen is that way. Bathroom is there. And the bedroom is just through those doors."

One bedroom?

Rae's eyes flickered to him automatically and he was quick to explain.

"Our cover identities are Blaine and Meg Rosswell. Newlyweds from Sussex. One bedroom made sense if anyone was to check."

She couldn't help but frown. "Will anyone check? Is anyone on the lookout for us tonight?"

"No," he shook his head, "at least, no one that we know of. But we can never be too careful. Especially after...recent events." A shadow passed over his face and before he could stop himself he added, "I want to keep you safe."

They shared a long look, before Rae finally provided him a graceful exit. "For the mission?"

His face broke into a grateful grin and he chuckled softly. "Yeah, for the mission."

"Well, on behalf of the Privy Council, I thank you for your consideration." She couldn't help but grin herself as she pointed to one of the doors. "Bathroom?" He nodded. "Cool. I'm going to take a shower before the thing tonight."

He nodded again, but called out to her before she disappeared. "Rae, just...remember it starts at six o'clock. That's just a little over an hour from now."

She paused in the doorframe and turned around suspiciously. "What's that supposed to mean?"

His face was a perfect mask of innocence. "Nothing."

"Then why did you say it?"

"I'm just reminding you, is all."

She folded her arms across her chest with a wry smile. "And would you remind Julian, if he was your partner right now instead of me?"

Devon looked like he'd backed himself into a corner, but he handled it as gracefully as he could. "It's just...you tend to take longer showers and—"

"I knew it!" She pointed a finger at his chest in triumph. "You just can't let it go!"

He held out for just a second more before the jig was up. A wide smile spread across his face and he chuckled again at her defiance. "...Longest showers of anyone I've ever known."

"I have a lot of hair!" she said defensively, tossing her long curls out behind her. "It's quite a bit of maintenance, I'll have you know!"

"I know exactly how much hair you have." He glanced up with a grin. "Your showers still last roughly seven years."

She threw up her hands, simultaneously conjuring a bottle of her favorite conditioner as she headed to the door. "You're so prone to over-exaggeration."

"I once started and finished watching *Scarface* in the time it took you to take a shower."

"Well," she sniffed, "I think that has a lot more to do with your bad taste in movies than it does with me relaxing in the shower."

He snorted. "Right."

She had halfway closed the door, when she turned around with a sudden grin. "You know...this conversation isn't that professional either."

He faltered a moment, before his face grew suddenly solemn. "Yes it is. I'll have you know, I had this exact same talk when I was stationed with Julian in Spain."

Rae rolled her eyes and closed the bathroom door, collapsing back against it with a grin.

Devon may be the Privy Council golden boy once again. He may be the man with all the answers, but he was struggling with this just as much as she was. And just like that, the path that lay ahead of her was suddenly clear.

A competition to be professional for the next twenty-four hours? Well, game on! She'd be as freakin' professional as they come.

She stared at herself in the mirror. With that being said...what was a competition without a little friendly sabotage?

After intentionally taking the quickest shower of her young life, Rae intentionally walked by Devon in a tiny towel and then disappeared into the bedroom, locking the door.

Devon had agreed to sleep on the couch—in keeping up with their one-bedroom appearances—and Rae hadn't argued. This was partially because the Savoy had the biggest, most extravagant-looking bed she'd ever laid eyes on, and partially because she needed some serious alone time to get ready for the party.

With a picture of the dress from the magazine Julian had pointed out taped up against the mirror, she lifted her hands and let the magic begin...

Just under an hour later, she slowly opened the door. Devon was sitting on a chair in the living room, reading a copy of the London Daily Telegraph. It lowered slowly in front of him as he stared out from over the top, his mouth falling open in unrestrained astonishment.

The dress she'd selected looked more like a skyline at dusk than anything she'd ever seen worn on a mannequin. It hugged her bodice in a tight sweetheart top, before flaring out into a full skirt, shaded in every color of the summer sunset. Swirls of coppery orange, burnt rose, and deep magenta melted together into one stunning ensemble—a walking work of art that seemed to almost glow as she took a tentative step forward.

"Well," her voice shook a little, as she found herself suddenly nervous, "what do you think?"

Devon's blue eyes dilated hungrily as the newspaper balled up in his hand. "*That's* keeping things professional?"

Her pulse pounded in her ears, and she felt the sudden need to put on a jacket. Or a blanket. Or maybe even the super-convenient parka she had tragically left at home. Her brilliant strategy had backfired in a wave of nerves, and her cheeks flushed as she smoothed down the fabric. "Julian knew what kind of place this was, so he told me what to wear..." And probably saw this exact moment happening, the psychic bastard. "Just give me two seconds and I'll change—"

"No," Devon said, a little quicker than was necessary. He caught himself and slowed things down with an easy smile. "You look...you look perfect."

She flashed him a shy smile, and he was quick to correct himself.

"For the mission. You look perfect for the mission."

For whatever reason, instead of chafing at his clarification she found herself smiling. "I do, don't I?" she teased, doing a little twirl. The feather-light fabric spun out in a graceful arch around her—creating their own little sunset, right there in the room.

Devon sucked in quick breath and dropped his eyes deliberately to the floor. "That's not fair," he muttered quietly.

"What was that?" she asked loudly, pretending not to have heard.

He looked up with a grin. "Nothing. Come on, let's get downstairs. There's a five-star party going on, and somewhere inside it a billionaire is waiting to get a tracer put on his jacket." He cleared his throat. "And I need a drink."

He opened the door and turned expectantly, but Rae was still standing right where he'd left her. When she caught his eye, she put her hands daintily on her hips, and dropped her head with a martyred sigh. "Devon Wardell, do I have to teach you *everything* there is to know about being a spy?"

His face blanked, and he shook his head in confusion. "What—"

"We're supposed to be a couple, aren't we...?" she asked patronizingly.

For a second, neither of them moved. Then he realized what she was talking about and crossed the room to take her arm.

"There you go, princess," he rolled his eyes but smiled, "is *that* better?"

She grinned victoriously and swung her purse towards the door. "Perfect! Let the undercover-mission-seeking-party begin!"

Chapter 8

It was a good thing that Rae wore a gown glowing with the vibrancy of seven suns, because if she hadn't it's likely she would have gotten lost in the crowd.

As the elevator doors opened, she and Devon joined a flood of people in a twinkling sea of diamonds and brightly-colored chiffon pouring down a winding staircase to get to the ballroom. She held on tightly to his hand, wishing for the millionth time in less than a minute that she hadn't worn such high heels. His tatù helped, lending her a balance that she otherwise lacked, but she still felt as though she was constantly teetering on the edge of disaster.

Story of my life, she thought to herself as she gripped his hand tighter trying to navigate the stairs.

Devon saw what she was doing, and tilted his head down to hers with a whisper he knew she would hear, "Hey, Rambo, ease up. Heightened strength, too, remember?"

Her face soured, and she held on just as hard. "It's not my fault. These things are a nightmare waiting to happen. I should never have listened to Julian. The dress, yes. The shoes... hell no!"

He stifled a grin. "So why did you?"

"Devon, please. You know how I like to be tall."

He rolled his eyes and pulled her suddenly into a side hallway, out of the tide of people, as soon as they reached the end of the staircase. She looked around in surprise, smoothing down her dress as he glanced quickly around for listening ears or cameras watching them.

"So remember," he murmured in a low voice, "Blaine and Meg Rosswell. We just got married three months ago, and honeymooned in France. If anyone asks what we're doing in London, we're here visiting your extended family before travelling back to Sussex."

Rae put her hands on her hips. She hissed quietly, "Devon, I did read the briefing book, you know."

"Jackman White is famous for dancing, drinking, and gambling. We'll catch him doing any one of those things, and use the opportunity to put the tracer on his jacket. The second we have, we'll head up to his office on the top floor to search for any communications between him and the Knights."

"Yeah...as I recall, that was on page four."

"We are to photograph only. Not remove the copies. Once we're finished, it's mission complete and back to base. Unless it's too late, in which case we have the room for the night."

She threw up her hands. "Devon, seriously, I read the—"

"Sometimes you just kind of skim through it," he interrupted apologetically.

Her mouth fell open in protest. "Devon—"

"Sometimes you use it as a coloring book."

She stomped down a heel, growing more and more frustrated the wider he smiled. "Would you stop! That was one time! I'd read through it already, and if you recall we were stuck sitting in that office for forty minutes while the Deputy Missions Commander took a phone call."

He nodded, looking falsely grave. "And I'm pleased to say you used that time as wisely as you could."

Her eyes flicked down to his starched white shirt, and narrowed with sinister possibilities.

He took a step back, lifting one hand protectively in front of it. "What?"

"Oh nothing," she smiled sweetly, "I'm just thinking of what else I can color on."

He took a giant step back and gestured to the staircase with a grin. "After you." As she passed in front of him, he couldn't help but add, "Careful with the heels."

"Bite me." She smiled despite herself.

They made their way down the ornate hall and into the ballroom with no further discussion, but once there, even Mr. Reads-the-mission-book-from-cover-to-cover couldn't fully mask his awe.

"This is incredible," he breathed, tilting his head up to peer at the spiraling murals on the vaulted ceiling. "I feel like I should be wearing a cape."

"Well, perhaps if you apologize for the heels comment, I can conjure you one later tonight." Rae lifted a glass of champagne off a passing tray with a gracious smile, extending her little finger automatically as she took a delicate sip.

Devon gave her a sideways grin, and just as graciously offered her his arm. "Shall we?"

"Sweep me off my feet with your crazy dance moves, *Blaine*."

As it turned out, even considering the number of people swirling away in the center of the dance floor, it wasn't hard to find Jackman White. For once thing, he easily dwarfed most of the people gathered around him—standing at what had to be close to seven feet tall—and if that wasn't enough, both Devon and Rae could hear his booming laugh from halfway across the room.

Rae lifted a hand to her ear with a wince. "And... switching out of your tatù now."

"Lucky," Devon muttered as they wandered casually closer.

White fit the stereotype of a billionaire playboy to a "T". He was about ten years older than them, maybe twenty-eight or twenty-nine, surrounded by a host of some of the most beautiful women Rae had seen in her life. Each one of them wore a similar couture gown and matching vacant expressions. Only White's roaring laughter cued them in as to when it was time to smile.

Maybe that's why he started doing it so loudly... "How exactly are we going to get close enough to put on a bug?" she asked quietly, eyeing the impenetrable crowd around him.

Devon considered for a moment, his ocean blue eyes taking note of every innocuous detail, before he came to rest on the bevy of girls. The corners of his lips turned up in a small smile that Rae couldn't quite understand, and he took her by the hand. "Come on," he said, taking her champagne and putting it on a passing tray, "let's dance. Again."

"Wait—*what*?"

Before she could object, Devon swept her along to the center of the floor, twirling her with an effortlessness that seemed almost otherworldly. At first she held on for dear life, but after slipping back into his ink, she found the experience much more enjoyable.

"So," she gasped, spinning out in a wide circle before coming back to him, "what exactly is the point of this? I thought we were supposed to be zeroing in on Jackman."

Devon grinned and spun her around again. This time he pulled her all the way back into his chest, catching her at the last second and holding her tight against his body. She could feel his heart pounding beneath his tuxedo, and the warmth from his skin sent a shiver up her spine.

"We are," he laughed. She caught her breath and stared up into his twinkling eyes. "Trust me."

The song ended, and another began. Not a moment later, Rae felt a soft tap on her shoulder. She looked around in surprise to see Jackman White standing there, looking her over with a hungry expression in his eyes.

"Excuse me," he said with the hint of a Southern drawl, "I don't mean to interrupt, but I couldn't help but noticing that you, young man, are dancing with the most beautiful woman in the room."

Rae's eyes flitted behind him to where his little harem stood sulking on the sidelines.

Jackman intercepted her stare with a self-important smile. "I only mention this because I make it a point to do that myself." He gave Devon a good-natured grin. "Looks like tonight I got beat."

Devon chuckled politely, and gripped Rae's hand. "I believe you did."

"Allow me to introduce myself." Jackman stuck his hand in between them, forcing Devon to let go. "My name's Jackman White. Visiting London all the way from big ol' Texas."

Devon shook firmly, whilst all the while Rae was completely ignored. *That fits. This guy thinks girls are trophies and property. It's no wonder he hasn't done anything but leer and grin like an idiot since he came over.*

"Blaine Rosswell," Devon answered confidently. "Pleased to meet you."

It happened so fast that even Rae, using Devon's own tatù, almost missed it. The way his hand swept under Jackman's arm, holding the tracer between two fingers. The way he pressed it so hard into the material, a moment later it had disappeared.

This was his plan all along, she realized with a start. *From the moment we started dancing.*

It wasn't a bad idea, she had to admit. After all, if the mountain wouldn't come to you, then... Her eyes narrowed as another key component clicked into place.

She was the bait.

Using every bit of strength from a particular clamp tatù she had, she squeezed his fingers to get his attention. "Honey, aren't you going to introduce me?"

He winced and gingerly extracted his hand, turning her towards Jackman with a pained smile. "My apologies. Mr. White—this is my wife, Meg."

"Your wife?" Jackman's voice boomed out over the ballroom. Despite his obvious intentions he didn't seem in the least bit put out by this information, but was rather intrigued. "You kids are a bit young to be getting married, aren't you?"

Devon's eyes flashed, but the next second he was under control. "What can I say?" He pulled Rae discreetly back towards him and wrapped an arm around her waist. "When you know, you know."

White threw back his head and laughed, causing the people dancing around him to jump in alarm. "Isn't that the truth! I've 'known' myself three or four times now, but I'm always on the lookout for the next Mrs. White." He threw Rae a wink whilst nudging Devon with a grin.

What could the Knights possibly want with him? What exactly does he think is going to happen tonight? That Devon'll give him permission to bed his new wife?

She had a feeling she wasn't far off the mark with that one.

"Mr. Rosswell," he said jovially, pre-emptively taking Rae's hand, "may I steal your wife away for a dance?"

Rae didn't need to hear it to know exactly what Devon was going to say next. He was going to refuse. Sure, he'd used her as bait to lure the guy over here, but he didn't have any intention of letting things go further than that. In fact, she got the feeling that he was going to relish saying no.

Except it really wasn't up to him, now was it? He'd used her as bait. The least she could do was return the favor.

"Mr. White," she cut Devon off, stepping forward with a radiant smile, "I would love to."

Devon froze, not quite letting go. "*Honey*, are you sure—"

"Would *love* to," Rae repeated, flashing him a smirk as White swept her away across the floor.

Jackman White may have all the money in the world, but dancing with him was nothing like dancing with Devon. There were far more near-misses and foot-stomps. Yet considering the man was the target of a Privy Council investigation, she didn't have a bad time.

He was all bravado and arrogance, sure. But he knew it. He also knew that she knew it. So in a way, it wasn't hard at all to have a relatively normal conversation... minus the fact that she was using a fake name in a magically conjured ball gown, and was about to break into his private study. Not that Mr. White needed to know that.

"So," he squeezed her hand and brought her a step closer, "how do you like being married?"

Her eyes flickered across the floor to where Devon was watching them with a clenched jaw. "It's...not quite what I expected."

"Oh? How so?" He spun her around, narrowly missing another couple, though he remained completely oblivious.

She righted herself with a quiet gasp. "Well—relationships are work, you know? Sometimes it's not so easy to see where all the lines are supposed to be drawn." She couldn't believe she was attempting to have this conversation right now. Truth be told, of all the people in her life right now with whom she could discuss Devon Wardell, this guy might actually be the most harmless. If nothing else, at least he wasn't biased.

He nodded effusively. "I completely agree. Just last week my girlfriend Kendra called me up, *furious* that she'd seen a tabloid cover of me kissing another woman."

Rae blinked in disbelief. On second thought, maybe not the greatest confidant.

"I know!" he cried, misunderstanding her entirely. "Unless things have been expressly stated, how am I supposed to navigate the inner workings of her mind?"

A wave of 'sisterhood' anger welled up in her chest, but Rae just bit her lip and looked down with a small smile. "*Women.*"

"Indeed!" He squeezed her hand even tighter, steering her back the way they'd come as the song wound to a close. "But not you, eh?"

She looked up in surprise to see him grinning down at her. Devon was already making his way towards them through the dispersing crowd, but White didn't seem to care.

"I'm sorry?"

What exactly was he trying to imply?

His eyes danced with another over-confident smile. "Oh no, I mean no disrespect. It's just that you—and your husband as well, for that matter—don't seem like a lot of the people I usually run into at these events. In fact, if you're amenable, I was hoping to make a little proposition..."

"A proposition...?" Rae took a step back and nearly melted with relief when she bumped into Devon, who had just reached them from across the room.

He wound both arms around her waist and pulled her into him, with a casual yet incredibly pointed smile. "What did I miss?" he asked testily, looking Jackman up and down.

Rae glanced over her shoulder with a strained smile. "Actually, Mr. White was just about to make some sort of—"

"I was wondering if you and your wife would like to join me and a few of my friends up in my suite later this evening."

Both Rae and Devon froze with twin looks of confusion.

"Your suite?" Devon repeated, trying and failing to understand.

White clapped him on the shoulder with an indulgent grin. "That's right. Just you, me, Meg, and a couple of the girls. We'll order up some champagne and make a night of it. What do you say?"

Rae was still completely lost, but it looked like Devon was beginning to catch on. His entire body stiffened and he stepped them both back out of reach.

"That's...quite an offer. But Meg and I actually have other plans. Thanks."

For the first time all night, White looked disappointed and stepped toward them. "Are you sure?" He flipped back a stray lock of Rae's hair then squeezed Devon on the shoulder. "I'm sure I could make it worth your while."

Rae had the fight the urge to throw a little Molly shock up this idiot's arm, followed by a stab of her stiletto. "Yep!" she answered in a high-pitched voice. "Totally sure!" She grabbed Devon by the wrist and backed them away into the crowd. "But...uh...thanks for the dance!"

They didn't stop moving until they were up the grand staircase and back in the elevator that led to the rooms. The second the door closed, they pulled away. When Devon turned to her with a disapproving scowl, Rae fell back against the wall in uncontrollable fits of laughter.

His glare turned to a look of utter astonishment as he watched her gasp for air. "What...the hell is wrong with you? Why are you *laughing* right now?"

"Devon," she hiccuped, wiping a tear from her face, "how are you *not* laughing right now?"

"He just—"

"Yeah—he just invited us to have some kind of drunken orgy." Another wave of giggles crumbled her back against the wall. "It's freaking hilarious! You should have seen your face!"

Devon failed to see the humor. "How the hell is it hilarious?! The man wanted to have sex with you!"

"And you!" Rae added, smoothing down her dress as she straightened up. "And like you're one to judge." Her smile sharpened dramatically. "Isn't that exactly what you were counting on when you swept me onto the dance floor?"

His cheeks flushed pink, and he realized he'd been caught. His dark hair spilled into his face as he bowed his head with a smile that showed that adorable dimple Rae was trying so hard to forget. "Alright, yeah. I knew he'd inevitably wander over and it'd be the perfect opportunity to place the bug. But I didn't want you to dance with him—let alone laugh at his offer for sex," he added quickly. "I didn't even want you to shake that asshole's hand..."

Rae shook her head, still grinning at the bizarre happenings of the night. Then something he said circled back to her, and she shot him an inquisitive glance. "Wait a sec. Why exactly did you think he would *inevitably* wander over? You saw all those girls circling around him. That seems like a pretty big chance to take, considering this is a mission and all."

Much to her surprise, Devon's face softened tenderly and he looked almost sympathetic.

"Come on, Kerrigan, when are you going to look in the mirror and see yourself clearly? You're ten times lovelier than any of those pathetic groupies. Having White see you dance was one of the only things I could count on tonight."

Rae's heart skipped a beat, and she lowered her face. *Way to keep things professional...*

This was exactly what she'd been talking about to Jackman. How the hell was she supposed to know where the lines were, when they'd been so irrevocably blurred? Here, she and Devon were supposed to be treating each other like agents, but then he goes and says something perfect like that? And look at her the way he was right now. *What on earth am I supposed to do with that?!*

"That's..." she cleared her throat and tucked her hair behind her ear. "Well, that's..." There was a *ding*, and she jerked her head up to see that they'd stopped at the top floor. She hadn't even seen Devon press the button, and now here they were. *Saved by the bell.* Go-time.

"You ready to earn your government paycheck?" he teased, looking at her with just the slightest bit of apprehension.

She turned around without the slightest hesitation. "Can you help me take off this dress?"

He froze. "Uh...what?"

"The zipper, Devon," she gestured impatiently. "Can you help me with the zipper?"

With incredibly hesitant hands, he pulled it down a couple of inches before she took over the rest. A moment later, she'd peeled off the gown entirely to reveal a sleek black jumpsuit underneath. It was leather and tightly fitted, perfect for this sort of reconnaissance. Sure, it didn't have sleeves like she would have preferred, but hey—fashion was pain, right?

"Alright," she gathered her hair into a ponytail, and secured it firmly in place, "ready."

He still didn't move.

"Devon," she said after another moment, gesturing to the door, "let's go."

"What?" He blinked then opened it in a rush. "Yeah, let's...let's go."

You know how some people say that you can tell a dog just by looking at its owner? Well, after meeting Jackman White—it was clear that they were standing in *his* office.

There wasn't an inch of the floor that wasn't littered with empty champagne bottles, cigar ash, scattered bits of lingerie, and enough empty tins of caviar to feed a small army.

Rae picked through it in disgust. "Didn't he only get in, like, two days ago?"

"The man likes to party," Devon answered, glancing discreetly away as he moved a rhinestone bra to the side with his shoe. "Something you were given the chance to see up close and personal tonight, if you had so desired."

"Damn," she snapped her fingers, "just my luck."

While Devon checked behind the paintings hanging on the wall for a mounted safe, Rae made a beeline for the desk. It was locked—big surprise—but thanks to Ethan's conjuring ink, she had only to look at the bolt before the key appeared in her hand.

"Dev," she called, rifling through the first few files, "I think I have something over here."

There was a blur of color, then he was kneeling by her side.

"Mallins was right," he said in mild surprise. "This guy has been bankrolling Xavier Knight operations for the last seven years."

"You didn't think he had?" Rae asked, taking out her phone and snapping a few pictures.

"Honestly..." Devon shook his head. "He didn't seem like the type. The man's a Texan billionaire. What does he care what a bunch of supernatural English freaks do with their time?"

Rae giggled and continued snapping pictures as he flipped through the files. "He doesn't have a tatù. I'd have picked it up when I shook his hand."

"According to the files, neither does anyone in his family. I've no idea how he could have gotten involved with something like this."

She photographed the last page and slipped the memory card into her pocket. "Well, you know who we could ask, don't you?"

Devon stared for a minute, before abruptly shaking his head. "No, we can't involve Luke."

"Why the hell not? He wouldn't mind." In the back of her mind, she knew it wouldn't be fair to ask him.

"We may be his friends, but that's his job, Rae. I'm sure he'd tell us if we were in any sort of danger, but whether he's dating Molly or not, we're on different sides." He didn't mention when Rae dated him very, very briefly, but somehow she knew he was thinking it.

Rae scoffed. "If it can help us... it wouldn't hurt to ask. He'll say no if it's information he can't share."

Devon shook his head. "We're not asking." When Rae opened her mouth, he cut her off before she could speak. "Not to mention, Carter isn't the only one who's going to be checking our mission reports from now on. Do you want to be the one to explain to Mallins how we found out confidential Knights information? Risk Luke getting into trouble? Losing his job?"

"Uh...I'll take a pass."

"That's what I thought." He grinned, locking the desk as he shut it. "Now, if we can just get to the door without disturbing White's labyrinth of debauchery, I think we're in the clear—"

No sooner had he spoken than a metallic *beep* only Rae and Devon would hear sounded from the hall. In what felt like slow motion, they both looked up in horror to see the lock on the door slowly turn.

Rae didn't have time to think. Didn't have time to plan. She didn't even have time to consider how extremely awkward this next part would be.

All she had time to do was grab Devon by the arms and dive underneath the bed.

Chapter 9

"What the hell are you doing?!"

Rae clapped a hand over Devon's mouth and froze. Together, the two of them peered out from the shadows to see one pair of heavy shoes and two pairs of stilettos stumble drunkenly into the room. There was the sound of high-pitched giggling, followed by White's booming laugh.

This is bad...on so many levels.

Over the last few years, Rae had been *in* bed with Devon. She'd yet to be *underneath* one. It was an entirely different experience.

As the feet tripped and teetered their way towards the bar, Rae glanced down for the first time. She was lying completely on top of Devon, her body pressed tightly against his with one hand still pressed firmly over his mouth. Thank goodness for high beds and bed skirts. What if the damn hotel had just used a box and they hadn't been able to hide under it? She removed her hand with an apologetic grimace and switched into Maria's telepathy. *Sorry—there wasn't time for anything else. I didn't know what else to do...*

His eyes met hers and he nodded swiftly.

Then they both glanced down at their rather compromising position.

Sorry about that, too... Even her mental voice sounded embarrassed, she realized with humiliation. *But hey, we're supposed to be newlyweds, right?* His eyes met hers with a wry grin and she flushed a million shades of red. *I can try to move—*

But at that moment, White and his ladies took their party to the bedroom. There was a loud *thud* and the springs above their heads creaked and strained as the three drunks fell onto the bed.

Rae paled in fear and tried to shimmy to the side, but Devon's hands held her tight.

"Don't move," he mouthed, tapping his ear. "They'll hear."

She reluctantly obeyed, but as White rolled over on the mattress the springs caved in and the entire thing pushed into her back—pressing her even tighter into Devon. He wound his hands protectively around her so the metal wouldn't cut, and tried to make himself as small as possible to give her all the room he could.

It still wasn't very much.

Only in times of extreme intimacy had the two of them ever been this close. To be perfectly honest, Rae figured this was even a bit closer than that. So close it was almost painful. Not physically painful... but the other kind. The kind that needed what was going on top of the bed to fix.

They were cheek to cheek—Devon looking up, and Rae staring down—and their bodies were squeezed in so tight that they began automatically timing out their breathing. First one would breathe, then the other. There wasn't enough room for them both to do it at the same time.

After what seemed like an eternity, and accompanied by some disgusting kissing sounds, the trio shifted slightly and Rae was able to lift her head slightly. She drew in a silent breath of relief, but when she looked down she saw Devon grinning up at her.

What?! she asked, slipping back into the telepathy. *What the hell could you possibly be smiling at right now?!*

His eyes somehow twinkled even in the dark.

"Keeping things professional..." he whispered.

She bowed her head with silent laughter, touching their foreheads together. Then, regardless of the squeeze, Devon somehow managed to shift his arm around and lace his fingers through hers.

Her eyes locked onto him in surprise, watching as he rubbed gentle circles on her knuckles with his thumb. He took his time, ignoring her pointed stare as he stroked up and down, re-exploring the same hand he'd held for years.

What...was this now?

A tiny shiver ran up her spine and she bit her lip and turned her head, ashamed that he'd be able to feel it. A pair of fingers caught her gently below the chin and turned her back. He shook his head thoughtfully, while his eyes silently asked her to stay.

She could hardly breathe. She could hardly think. All she could do was stare back at him, wondering what in the world was going on inside that beautiful head of his.

Then, before she could ask, there was the sound of ripping fabric followed by a dull groan.

Devon closed his eyes with a wince, while Rae buried her face in his chest.

Please, oh please. If I've stored up any amount of good karma, let me use it now. Let this not be happening.

She wasn't sure if she'd projected the thoughts or not, but either way Devon shook beneath her with stifled laughter. The moaning picked up, as did the breathing, and the springs above their heads squeaked with sickening regularity.

When one of them jabbed her ferociously in the back, she looked down at him and bit back a cry. Her healing tatù quickly fixed the pain.

Worst. Mission. Ever.

He shrugged, and lowered his voice to a mischievous whisper. "It has its perks." His fingers squeezed hers softly, and she realized he was still holding her hand.

They lay there for a while longer, enduring it as best they could. She was warm, hotter on the inside than out. It didn't help that the bed motion above them was hitting her hips and pressing them into Devon in a consistent, rhythmic pattern. She ran her tongue over her top lip and watched Devon's eyes drop down to her mouth. Did he want to kiss her as badly as she wanted to kiss him? She pressed her lips lightly together and saw him swallow hard. Screw it! All she had to do was move her head slightly, and their lips would touch. Chemistry would take over the rest of it. They could deal with the repercussions later. One kiss. Just one taste of his tongue in her mouth. She closed her eyes and—

"How about it, sexy ladies? Shall we continue this in the shower?" White's voice seemed right beside Rae's ear.

She popped her eyes open and sighed in relief as the bed shifted and bumped. A second later, three pairs of feet shuffled quickly to the bathroom. Not taking any chances, Rae stayed perfectly still until the sound of laughter and running water drowned out any noise she and Devon could possibly make. When the trio was finally in full swing, she pushed herself tentatively to the side.

Two hands stopped her.

Her eyes snapped back to Devon in a question, but he was staring at her with an expression so intense she honestly had no way to interpret it. Keeping his eyes on her all the while, he turned his head a little so their lips were even closer than before.

There wasn't a sound between them, save for the whisper of shallow breathing. In fact, the entire world seemed to fade away as they stared into each other's eyes.

Then he lifted his head, and kissed her.

They were able so slip out of the penthouse with relative ease, and even though they still had the room rented for the night, neither one of them seemed particularly eager to stay. It was as though just the thought was an unexpected pressure, looming over the both of them.

Would they? Wouldn't they? Didn't that effectively demolish the idea of agent boundaries?

The questions were all settled decisively when they began packing immediately upon returning to their room.

As Rae tossed handfuls of clothes into her bag—the bag it felt like she had just started packing a few hours before—she replayed it over and over again in her mind.

The way he'd leaned forward and slipped his hand into her hair. The ways his lips had parted hers with expert familiarity. The way the kiss had deepened like the most natural thing in the world, and the way their bodies had melded together.

But that's not the whole story, Rae, she told herself firmly. *Play it through.*

And she was right. Because while the kiss itself might have been perfection, the second they pulled apart everything started to unravel...

She recalled the look in Devon's eyes as he'd stared up at her. It was as if he was being literally torn in two. A part of him wanted nothing more than to keep going, but another part, just as strong, pulled away. Although he had initiated the whole thing, he seemed as caught off guard by his behavior as she was, and the second they were free of the bed he couldn't get away fast enough.

Even as she heard the frantic sounds of his packing, she wondered if he was regretting his decision. It wasn't like the thing had been planned. And it certainly didn't follow along with their new strategy of 'professionalism to a fault.'

"Rae?"

She jumped a mile at the soft voice, and turned around to see him standing nervously in the doorway. "Hey..." she tucked her hair behind her ears. "Sorry; you scared me."

He took a deep breath and glanced down at the bed, avoiding her eyes. "So I think it's probably best we just head back tonight. Is that cool with you?"

"Well, yeah," she glanced down at her suitcase. "I was kind of planning on it."

His eyes snapped up sharply. "You were?"

"*You* certainly were," she shot back accusingly.

It hung in the air between them for a moment, then they let it go.

"I'll get the car and meet you downstairs," he said, sighing.

"That's fine," she replied in the same soft monotone.

Then he was gone.

She stared at the door for a long while after he'd left, wondering how, in this crazy 'professional' mission, things had gone so far off the rails. How were they going to get back on track?

The ride back to Privy Council had never seemed so long. It was long after midnight by the time they finally pulled into Guilder, but all the lights in the Oratory were still on. Rae followed Devon inside without a word, the pictures she'd taken tucked safely into her bag. She didn't know exactly how they were going to debrief on this one, but she was content to let him take the lead. With any luck, Mallins wouldn't press too hard.

"Well, good evening."

Both she and Devon froze in their tracks as they pushed open the door to find Carter, not Mallins, sitting behind the mahogany desk.

"I wasn't expecting you two until tomorrow morning." He stood up to greet each of them before gesturing them to sit. "To be honest, I wasn't expecting you two to be sent out on a mission together at all, but I'm sure Victor had his reasons..."

Despite his gesture to sit, she and Devon were still frozen in place. Their eyes widened as both wondered the inevitable question: For *this* particular mission, might it have been better to have Mallins? After everything they'd been through, Carter knew them both a little too well.

"Sit," he repeated, eyeing their reluctant posture curiously. "You've both done this before. It looks like we have a lot to go over. Let's start at the beginning."

Rae and Devon flashed each other a quick look, taking a seat and angling as far away from each other as possible. They were silent for a moment, both waiting for the other to begin, until Carter finally threw up his hands.

"Someone speak!"

Devon cleared his throat nervously. "We arrived at the Savoy, got ready for the event, and proceeded straight to the ballroom. Once we identified Jackman White, we maneuvered ourselves close enough that I was able to put on the tracer. Then we headed up to his office and proceeded to go through the papers we found there."

At this point, Rae silently handed the photos across the desk to Carter.

"As you can see," Devon continued, "Mr. White has been funding the Xavier Knights for quite some time. I suspect that he inherited it from his father, and his father before him, and so on."

"Excellent." Carter nodded brusquely, flipping through the pictures. "Any problems?"

Devon faltered. "I'm sorry, sir?"

With the expression of someone who didn't miss much, Carter glanced up and fixed both teenagers firmly in his gaze. "I said...did you two have any problems? With the mission?"

Their eyes flicked to each other once again before both looked decidedly away.

"No sir," Devon said softly, "no problems."

Carter stared at them for a moment, before slipping the pictures in his desk. "Good. Well, if there's nothing further, then you're dismissed. I'll see you later this week for training."

Devon pushed to his feet, but Rae lingered there, staring at Carter imploringly. "Actually, sir, I was wondering if maybe I could talk to you for a minute?"

Carter frowned curiously as Devon froze by the door.

"Yes, of course, Miss Kerrigan. Mr. Wardell, I'll see you in a few days."

Devon's hands tightened on the knob, but he didn't move. "Uh, Rae—I'm your ride. Do you want me to wait, or...?"

Shit! Of course he is! I didn't think of that...

Rae froze in dismay, the whirlwind of emotions in her head prohibiting her from landing on a single coherent thought.

Fortunately, in an act of sheer mercy Carter stepped in and saved the day. "That won't be necessary, Devon," he answered, fixing Rae gently in his eyes. "I can give her a ride back to London. In fact," he stood up and got his coat, "we can talk in the car."

The three of them walked out of the Oratory in awkward silence, each one not quite understanding what exactly was going on. The second they were in view of the parking lot, Devon gave them a quick nod goodbye and vanished through the trees. Cater stared after him with a slightly worried expression before turning back to Rae.

"Do you want me to ask again...were there any problems tonight?"

Rae had to hand it to him: Carter didn't press. In fact, when she again denied that anything had gone overtly wrong on their mission, he let it go without another word. And this was coming from a man who could simply touch her skin and know the truth.

She slid gratefully inside his car and buckled her seatbelt, sniffing around at the smell of softened leather. It was one of those luxury vehicles that was just as expensive as Devon and Julian's prized sports cars, but was suited to a slightly older man. He climbed in beside her and revved the engine. A minute later, they were flying down the country roads to London.

"So," he finally asked as they veered off onto the interstate, "are you going to tell me what's on your mind? Or were you just looking for an excuse to escape Mr. Wardell's reckless driving?"

Rae tilted her head down with a smile of embarrassment. She hadn't realized how long she'd just been sitting there in silence.

Carter turned to her with infinite patience. "What's going on, Rae?"

She nervously chewed her lip. Where did she even begin? And how much of what she told Carter would end up getting back to her mom? "Does this stay between us?" she asked quietly. He turned to her in surprise. "I mean, do we have, like, agent-supervisor confidentiality or something?"

The car slowed down slightly and he twisted round with a look of concern. "Rae, what is it?"

She sighed. "I don't like Mallins being president." It was an innocuous enough way to begin, but the layers of complication wound up in that statement were too numerous to count.

Carter stared at her for a second more, before his lips tilted up in a hard smile. "Nor do I."

"He took me out to lunch the other week. Basically told me that for the good of everyone around me, I should shuffle off to the far corners of the earth. He flat out said he didn't know why in the world I would be a considering taking back my job with the Privy Council."

Carter gave her a sharp look. "He said that? He said *that*, and then he assigned you to work again with Devon?"

She nodded. "Yeah. He thinks I'm dangerous. He doesn't want me corrupting his precious agency."

They were quiet for a while, both thinking hard.

Finally, Carter turned back to the road with a sigh. "Well, fortunately it's not entirely up to him." He cast her a sideways glance. "But, Rae...I'm fairly sure that's not what you wanted to talk to me about."

Her face flushed guiltily and she dropped her eyes to her lap. Was she that easy to read? This was getting ridiculous. "I may have ...I made a little detour in Scotland."

His eyebrows raised, but he kept his eyes on the road. "Okay...?"

"Because I found a letter my father left for me back at the old farmhouse."

He flashed her a look, but said nothing.

"A letter that led me to this inn, that led me to this tree, that led me to this..." She shook her head, unable to handle Simon Kerrigan's eccentricities right now. "Well, long story short—*here.*"

She tossed him the final piece of the brainwashing device. The piece no one probably knew existed. Except her father. Could he have hidden it from Cromfield as well? She shook her head. That didn't make sense. Her father worked for the man. He left the Privy Council to follow him. Or be like him, or something.

She'd been carrying it around in her coat pocket ever since she got back, wondering what in the world she was going to do with it now that Mallins was in charge of the Privy Council. Now that she maybe, kind of, possibly *suspected* the Privy Council. But right there, sitting in the car with Carter, the answer was suddenly clear as could be.

Whether the Council was corrupt or not, Carter certainly wasn't. She realized that she would trust him with just about anything. She would trust him with this.

He caught it in surprise, and turned it over to see what it was. "Is this...?" His voice trailed off in shock. "Is this the—"

"It's the final piece," Rae finished. "I didn't want to give it to Mallins, so I've been hanging onto it for a while."

Carter was stunned. "You found this in Scotland?" She nodded silently, and he shook his head in wonder. "Rae, we hid four pieces. But this...this is different. No one in the world had any idea this existed or where it was buried. We've never been able to gather any credible intel as to its location."

She sighed again. "Well, now you've got it. I would just...be careful who you tell." Her voice dropped an octave and she stared out the window. "Never can quite tell who to trust these days."

There was a crunch of tires, and all of a sudden the car pulled to the side of the road.

Rae turned to Carter in alarm, but he was staring at her with that same calm attentiveness that over the years, she had come to expect.

"Rae Kerrigan," his voice was neither stern nor casual, but somewhere in the middle, "tell me what was in the letter."

She stared at him silently as cars whizzed past.

She'd already given him the piece; she might as well go the rest of the way. Of course, that didn't mean that he was going to like anything she had to say.

"He told me not to trust the Privy Council. He said that their record wasn't exactly spotless and that the whole organization wasn't as it seemed."

Carter nodded encouragingly as she hesitated to go forward.

"He told me to..." she faltered, "...to look into my grandparents. Which I did, and...I know this sounds crazy, but I don't think my dad killed them." She peered up tentatively, but Carter's face was unreadable. She couldn't tell if he was taking any of this seriously, or if he was preparing to haul her off for being as demented as dear old dad. "Anyway, I flew to New York to ask my uncle some questions and look them up, but I couldn't find much of any information. So..." This time she couldn't go forward. How was she supposed to sit in the President of the Privy Council's car and confess that she was about to perpetrate a crime?

Carter inclined his head and caught her eye. "So...?"

Her shoulders stiffened, and she decided just to go for it. "So I decided to become an agent again, so that I'd have access to the PC mainframe and I could try to find out what really happened to them." She said it all in one breath, and found her hand half-reaching for the door—preparing for an escape should one become necessary. The locks snapped down.

Her eyes flashed up in fear, but Carter was smiling gently. "Well, it's not exactly what I wanted to hear, but I can't say that I'm surprised. After all, it's been a few weeks now since you've gotten into some sort of mischief—I guess you're due."

"You guess I'm...?" Rae couldn't believe her ears. Was Carter actually okay with this?

"Who's helping you?" he asked suddenly. She froze guiltily, and he rolled his eyes. "I don't believe for a second that this is something you're doing alone. So tell me now. Is it the whole crew? The fearsome-foursome back in action? Your mother?"

She bit her lip, but as he hadn't yet called in the armed guards, she didn't see the harm in telling him. "Just Julian."

He looked vaguely surprised. "Just Julian? No one else?"

Devon's face floated across her mind, and she shook her head firmly. "No one else. I didn't even want to involve Jules, but he saw it happening."

Carter nodded. "Of course he did." There was a spray of gravel, and the car eased slowly back onto the road. "Well, Rae, I'm not going to encourage you in this, but I'm not going to discourage you either. I would only caution you not to get your hopes up."

Have I entered some sort of parallel universe?!

"Sir," she began cautiously, "of course I need to thank you for that, but..."

"But?"

She swiveled her body around to stare at him full on. "But why on earth aren't you having me arrested—again? I just told you that I'm going to break into the PC to steal confidential files."

Carter looked at her for a moment, then sighed. "Rae, I'm not trying to stop you because I know what you're going to find." His voice grew unexpectedly soft. "Simon killed them. I'm sorry to say it so bluntly, but it's true. Then again, if that's something that you need to find out for yourself, I completely understand. And I won't try to get in your way."

Rae sat there for a minute as the heavy implications of that statement sank in. She was grateful, for sure, but something about the resigned way he said it made her suddenly afraid.

"Sir, if I do happen to find out something different...would you like me to let you know?"

He chuckled softly. "Miss Kerrigan, by now I'd expect nothing different. Just don't say I didn't warn you if it doesn't go how you'd like."

She nodded slowly. "I won't."

The road flashed by as he veered off towards her apartment. They were just rounding the corner of the park, when he turned back to her suddenly. "And Rae?"

"Yes, sir?" She could have sworn he flashed her a wink.

"Don't get caught this time..."

Chapter 10

"I can't believe you!"

Julian paced back and forth in front of the sofa, waving his hands as he cursed under his breath.

Rae, meanwhile, sat calmly on the center cushion, trying to project an air of serenity. "Jules," she tried to be pragmatic, "I only told *one* person."

He whirled around on her, looking fierce. "The President of the Privy Council! You told the *President of the Privy Council!*"

"Yeah...he was the one..."

"I don't understand." He sank onto the sofa beside her, dropping his face into his hands. "Do you *want* us to get caught?!"

"*No*," she said emphatically. "Actually, I've been told specifically not to do that this time."

He shot her an equally impressive look of malice. "I'm in serious danger of trying to actually *kill* you, Kerrigan."

"Hey, buddy," Rae patted him tentatively on the back, "what happened to, 'you're like a sister to me, Rae. We're family.' What happened to that?"

"I got past it."

She dropped her hand. "Julian—"

"I can't see what's going to happen; you know that, right?" He looked up seriously. "There are too many variables at play."

"Nothing's going to happen," Rae stressed for the millionth time. "Look, it's simple. We break into the Oratory, head down one of the tunnels, steal a classified file, and take it back to—"

"Whoa—wait," he held up a hand to stop her, "what are you talking about?"

She leaned back suspiciously. "What are *you* talking about?"

"If neither one of you know what you're talking about, could I recommend the both of you simply shut up?!" Angel shouted from the next room. "I'm trying to watch TV in here."

Rae looked up with a frown, and Julian rolled his eyes.

"She never had television as a child. Big surprise, Cromfield didn't keep one in the bat-cave. I can't get her off Netflix."

Rae grinned. "Aw—poor baby." Finally, a normal problem. Well, minus the backstory about the cave...

He shot her a withering look. "It's not funny. Between that and your early morning wake-up calls, my sex life is taking a serious hit."

Rae dropped her eyes guiltily and chewed on her lip. She had scaled the wall and climbed up to his balcony this morning so as to avoid waking Devon by accident in the house. Needless to say, it had been an unfortunate repeat of the previous morning's interruption.

"If it helps, you two look really good together—"

"Please. Don't. Don't try to make it better." He closed his eyes with a painful expression.

She nodded swiftly. "Got it. Why don't we just stick to the plan?"

"I think that would be for the best."

She gave him a playful nudge and he opened his eyes with an exasperated grin.

"So, when I said we're going to break into the Privy Council to steal a confidential file," she repeated, "you weren't expecting to break into the Privy Council and steal a confidential file?"

He leaned back and shook out his hair. "No. Partially because I swore I'd never do that again, and partially because the files you're talking about won't be confidential. They're open to every agent with code-word clearance to read."

Rae's mouth fell open. Was there a handbook somewhere that no one had ever bothered to tell her about? *"Really?"*

"Yeah. The only rule is that you can't make any copies. Because of that, people generally just read them right there in the reference center, and then put them back."

"We have a *reference center*?"

"Devon was right." He paused. "You kind of just sit there and color until it's time to go, don't you?"

Rae ignored the comment. "So we just ask for the files on my grandparents and read them in the reference center? That's it?"

Julian grinned. "Yeah, genius. Not everything is scaling walls and smoke grenades. A lot of what we do is actually done on paper."

A wretched exercise she had apparently been able to avoid thus far. Rae shot him a devilish wink. "Where's the fun in that?"

He got to his feet. "I'm going to pretend like you didn't say that so I can get back to trying to reclaim my girlfriend from "Grey's Anatomy", or "Lost", or whatever it is she's stuck on now."

A voice from the other room piped up, "It's "Scandal"!"

"Ooh," Rae's eyes lit up, "that's a good one!"

Julian rubbed his face. "You two are going to be the end of me."

Rae giggled and got to her feet. "So we'll go this afternoon?"

"Cool. Fine. Whatever."

She shot him a disparaging look and he threw up his hands.

"SEX, Rae! I'd like to have SEX with my long-lost girlfriend. Vámonos!"

"Got it. Right. No problem." She gathered up her purse and headed to the door. But halfway out, she stopped suddenly and leaned against the frame. Devon wasn't home, so the wall-scaling thing had kind of been in vain. "Just one more thing."

"Rae..."

"Last night at the Savoy, there was this moment where Devon and I kind of—"

"Okay. Look." He put his hands on her shoulders, kneeling down to look her in the eye with a strained, big-brotherly kind of patience. "You can either keep interrupting me and Angel, or I can have a girly talk with you about Devon. You can't do both."

She hesitated, biting her lip. "I can't make promises either way..."

His eyes narrowed. "Going to KILL you, Kerrigan..." Then he shoved her out the door.

Having burnt one bridge long before breakfast, Rae decided to go try out another by seeing what Molly was up to at seven a.m. They hadn't had much of a chance to talk since Rae's return from New York and Scotland. To be honest, Rae argued with herself, Molly was so wrapped up in Luke these days she doubted Molly even noticed.

This time, she knocked long and hard on the other side of the door, and waited until she heard a bright, "Come on in!" before entering.

Molly was sitting in a beam of sunlight by her vanity, wrapped snuggly in her favorite purple cashmere robe. Her face lit up when Rae slipped inside. "Hey! Long time no see, stranger! Where did you slip off to this morning? I think you left before the sun was even up! You're not trying to write early morning poetry again, are you? Because I know that was just for a week or so back at Guilder, but even then I thought it was bad idea. And you know what they say: what's a bad idea back at Guilder is still a bad idea now. So seriously, what were you doing? And why don't you just tell me! Honestly, Kerrigan, you're so secretive these days, it's like pulling teeth just to get you to talk!"

As had become their custom, Rae waited patiently for Molly to take her first breath. The fresh supply of oxygen seemed to revive her, and she shot Rae another bright smile. "It is a good morning, eh?"

Rae laughed and settled herself down on the bed. "It is! Have you eaten yet—I'm absolutely starving."

"Not yet." She turned back to the mirror and smeared on a new shade of lip gloss. "I've been busy doing...other things."

She winked dramatically and Rae rolled her eyes.

"I mean *sex*."

"Yeah—yeah, I got it." She pulled a pillow into her lap and began tugging petulantly on the fringed edge. "Let me tell you something: you never realize how much fun all the couples around you are having until you're no longer part of a couple."

Molly swiveled around, looking something between smug and sympathetic. "Oh, honey...you and Devon are going to get back together any day now. All of us are just waiting for it to happen." She turned back to the mirror with a slight frown. "Julian says we need to make it sooner rather than later, because apparently you keep showing up at the crack of dawn and walking in on—"

"Yeah, about that," Rae cut her off, not eager to relive the awkward moment. "You know Devon and I were sent on a mission together last night?"

Molly turned back around. "Yeah, I heard. How'd it go?"

"Well, it was actually a little weird. So before we went, he gave me this whole big speech about how we were supposed to treat each other like agents and act strictly professional, right?"

Molly nodded, eyes wide, hanging on every word: The exact reaction Rae had been asking of Julian, who predictably refused.

This is why girls make better friends...

"Well, everything was going fine until we got cornered in this guy's hotel room and had to hide under the bed so he wouldn't catch us breaking into his desk."

"Were you naked?!" Molly interrupted with a gasp.

Rae paused mid-sentence. "Were we—*what*? Why would we have been naked?"

Molly shook her head, covering her mouth in anticipation. "It just seems that's the way these things always end up happening, right?"

Rae rolled her eyes. "Calm down, Nicholas Sparks, we weren't naked. However..." It seemed rather trivial after all that, but she couldn't help but share. "...he held my hand."

Molly pursed her lips. "He held your hand?"

"Yeah," Rae nodded seriously, "he did."

The tiny redhead paused a moment before venturing, "Rae, are you that lonely, or—"

"I'm saying, he gave me this big speech about professionalism, but when we were lying together under the bed he reached up and took my hand. And then he...he kissed me."

Molly almost fell out of her chair.

"He *did*?! Rae! Why didn't you call me?!"

Rae shook her head with a chuckle. "We were trapped under a bed while our target cavorted around with two supermodels...on the bed we were under. You wanted me to call?"

"Okay—so why didn't you *text* me?!"

Rae laughed again, then brought her knees up to her chest. "I just...I don't know what to do about him. We're broken up, I get that and, one way or another, we both need a little space. It's just...he *kissed* me, Molls. What am I supposed to do with that?" Should she tell Molly she had been on the verge of kissing him?

Molly scooted her chair closer to the bed, nodding with eyes wide as saucers. "Well, what did he do after he kissed you? Did he say anything? Did you guys talk about it?"

Rae's face darkened. "He didn't say a word. And the second we were out of there, he took off as fast as he could to get away from me. We didn't even end up staying the night at the hotel, even though we were probably technically supposed to."

Molly raised her eyebrows. "Not a single word?"

"Not a single word. The whole drive back to Guilder. He was the one who initiated, and now he's treating me like some kind of pariah! Won't even get close to me!" Should she mention she'd been kind of acting the same way?

"*Wow*," Molly said softly, brow furrowing together as she tried to interpret the confusing world of men. "Well, he's clearly still head over heels in love with you. That much is totally obvious."

Rae shook her head sarcastically. "*Is* it obvious? You know, seriously, I'm beginning to wonder. He's just been so weird lately. Like a whole different person. And not just with me, either, but with Julian, too. He told Julian he'd be debriefing on the Collins case a couple days ago, but he wasn't. He was in the library."

Molly tried and failed to look interested. "Okay, you had me up until the Collins case."

"But Molly, he—"

"Who cares? He probably just finished and then went to the library. This kiss, however, is another thing all together." Her face sharpened with almost cartoonish focus. "One on which I must use all of my not inconsiderable powers to solve..."

Before Rae could say a word to temper her enthusiasm, the door to the bathroom burst open and Luke walked out in a cloud of steam.

For a split second, nothing else in the room mattered.

His skin was glowing, his light hair dripped down the sides of his neck, and little trickles of water navigated their way slowly around the chiseled muscles on his chest and stomach.

Rae followed their progress all the way down to the towel which clung precariously around his hips, before his throat cleared suddenly and her cheeks flushed red with humiliation.

"Good...uh...good morning!" she deflected, averting her gaze to the wall.

Luke looked just as embarrassed as she was, gripping the towel with both hands like he was terrified it was going to fall off. "Yeah, uh...good morning."

The only one who seemed perfectly content with the way things were going was Molly, who swiveled around in her chair to give him a languid smile. "Hey, babe! Have a good shower?"

He bit his lip, but returned her smile indulgently. "Yeah. You, uh, you didn't want to maybe shout and tell me that there was someone lying on our bed before I came inside?"

Molly shrugged, looking completely unconcerned. "I forgot." The next second, she swiveled around again and whispered to Rae with a conspiratorial grin, "I didn't forget. I just wanted you to see how totally hot he looks with his shirt off."

Rae looked down and fought back a smile as Luke crossed his arms self-consciously over his chest, looking highly affronted.

"I am not a piece of—"

"Sure you're not, sweetie!" Molly interrupted cheerfully. "Want to do a little twirl for us?"

His eyebrows shot up, as he took a step forward. "Oh, you think this is funny?"

Molly braced automatically, and glanced around for an exit. "No," she giggled, "no I—"

"Then how about a little kiss?" He leaned down over her chair, fencing her in, and shook out his wet hair all over her face, giving her a sloppy kiss in the process.

She collapsed in a fit of threats and giggles, trying to ward him off as Rae shook her head like a martyr.

"This is exactly what I was talking about. The second I'm single, everyone else is in love."

Luke chuckled and pulled away, leaving Molly gaping in dismay at her reflection in the vanity mirror. "That's right. So how's it going then with you and Devon? Any progress?"

Molly paused in her damage-control efforts long enough to interject, "There was a *kiss*!"

"*Really*?" Luke raised his eyebrows good-naturedly as he fumbled around in the dresser, looking for clothes. "A whole kiss, huh?"

Rae glared at the both of them. "Yeah, there was a kiss." She focused the glare far more on Molly, who was frantically re-curling her hair. "Which was supposed to be *secret*, by the way."

Molly was far too distracted by her reflection to take notice, but Luke laughed again as he slipped on a shirt. His fingers twirled in the air, and Rae looked away as he pulled on jeans as well.

"Well, your secret is safe with me." He raked his fingers through his wet hair, then decided it was done and settled next to Rae on the bed. "Contrary to what you ladies think; we guys really couldn't care less about your relationship dramas."

Rae gave him an icy look, and even Molly turned slowly away from the mirror, looking dangerous. He back-pedaled in a hurry.

"I mean...when did this magical kiss happen, Rae?"

She jutted up her chin, but decided to tell him anyway. "It happened last night when we were paired up on a mission." A sudden beam of illumination struck her and she continued on carefully. "A mission where we were asked to check out a guy named Jackman White."

She raised her eyebrows knowingly, but Luke kept a perfect poker face. "Jackman White, huh?" He pretended to be puzzled. "Weird name."

Rae pursed her lips. "Yeah, that's what I thought, too." She leaned back on the pillows in defeat. "So you're really not going to tell me anything about him?"

"Nope." Luke kept his smile fixed on the bed. "But I also won't tell the people I work for that a Privy Council agent was asking about it, how about that?"

She shot him a rueful grin. "Fair enough. It was just me anyway. Scratch that. The Knights might not appreciate a Kerrigan digging." He gave her a playful shove, and she gracefully changed the subject. "So you've been working out with Devon, huh?"

"See!" Molly grinned triumphantly. "Those abs really make an impression, huh?"

Rae rolled her eyes. "I saw the two of them heading out to the gym the other day." She turned her gaze to Luke. "Seems you've found a new work-out buddy."

He scoffed. "That's one way of putting it."

Rae frowned sympathetically. "Hey, the guy has, like, built-in steroids." She gestured on her arm to where Devon was inked. "Don't take it personally."

"No, that's not what I meant," Luke said quickly. "The problem is he never stays there for more than like twenty minutes."

"What?"

"Yeah. Then he says he was some weird appointment or something else to do, and bails out every time." Luke shook his head thoughtfully. "I don't get it. I mean, we have fun when we're hanging out. And he's always the one to suggest it..."

Molly scoffed and turned back to the mirror. "Contrary to what you guys think; we ladies really couldn't care less about your relationship dramas."

He chuckled and the two of them struck up a teasing banter, but Rae couldn't get past what she'd just heard.

Why would Devon continually ask Luke to go to the gym with him, only to end up cutting it short every time? Where was he really going instead? The same place he'd snuck out to when he lied to Julian's face?"

"Rae?"

She looked up to see Molly and Luke looking at her strangely.

"Yeah? Sorry, what?"

Molly grinned. "I said, do you want to come and see a movie with us later?"

All at once Rae pushed to her feet, a flood of investigatory adrenaline pumping through her veins. "Actually, I'd love to but I can't. I'm meeting Julian at Guilder, and I should probably get ready." She skipped to the door and waved. "But thanks! And...uh...looking good, Luke!"

There was a burst of laughter behind her as the door swung shut.

Picking up speed, she raced to her room and started getting dressed.

One mystery at a time. First she'd find out whatever was in the file about her grandparents. And then she could turn her attention back to Devon...

Chapter 11

Rae took time to dress as inconspicuously as she could before meeting Julian in the reference center. They might not technically be doing anything wrong, but it would take but a nudge for the whole thing to go spinning out of control and land them somewhere they didn't want to be.

This is prison paranoia talking, she told herself as she swept nervously through the double doors. *This is what comes from having spent time in the 'big house.'*

Nevertheless, she had taken certain wardrobe precautions and was feeling pretty damn confident about her ability to project complete and utter innocence.

"Hey!" she greeted Julian warmly as she spotted him beside a table. "You ready for some good old-fashioned, legal fun?"

His eyes drifted up to her forehead, before returning dubiously to her face. "A headband?"

She fidgeted nervously. "I wear headbands sometimes. Nothing wrong with headbands."

"No, of course not." He pursed his lips. "It's just...you kind of look like the leader of the GSUSA – the Girl Scouts of the United States of America."

Her eyes narrowed into a scowl. "That's kind of the point, smartass. I'm blending in. No one ever suspects the Girl Scouts of the United States of America, now do they? And how do you even know what that is, anyway? Aren't you from Liverpool?"

He made a noble effort to keep from laughing. "How did they let you graduate?"

"Hey," she shot back, "at least I'm not trying to bed a girl who's more interested in the season finale of "Dexter"."

He shook his head and guided her gently towards the front desk. "It's like there's crack in those shows. I swear she hasn't slept in like four days..."

His face cleared into a charming smile as they came to a stop in front of the receptionist. She had to be at least four or five hundred years old. And even as Julian flashed her his most winning look, the wrinkles around her eyes deepened in distrust.

"What do you want?" she barked, beady eyes flashing between the two of them.

Julian fell back a step as his smile faltered. "Hi, Janice. How's your day going?"

"I said, what do you want?"

Both teenagers blinked as she sprayed them with an angry wave of spit.

Rae resisted her body's instinctive urge to become invisible, while Julian wiped his face and maintained a composed smile. I'd like Sophia Tresseux, Bill and Melanie Hilton, Peter and Katerina Kerrigan, and Laurence Funnel, please."

He lumped in Rae's grandparents along with a few of his other active cases. It was a good strategy, but one that the inscrutable Janice was able to see through almost immediately.

"Won't that be a little awkward?" she croaked, fumbling around a file cabinet. She cocked her head towards Rae in a pointed stare. "With *her* sitting right there with you?"

Rae opened her mouth to say something sarcastic, but Julian caught her elbow beneath the counter, and answered with a graceful smile. "She thrives on controversy. We'll be fine."

Janice peered at Rae over the top of her spectacles. "I guess she'd sort of have to." She left the room and came back ten minutes later with files in her hand. Rae resisted the urge to talk or look at Julian while they waited. Who knew what kind of cameras were in this place? Janice walked in with the files, appearing not even to notice their weight. "Well, here's everything you wanted." She handed him a stack of papers. "Anything else?"

Again, he squeezed her arm and Rae stepped forward. "Yeah, can I have the background file on Jackman White, please?" She had no intention of going through it, but figured it gave her a plausible reason for being there if anyone were to ask.

"White...White..." Janice disappeared for a moment before plopping a heavy manila envelope into Rae's hand. "There you go—enjoy."

"Thanks, Janice," Julian said politely as they both innocently backed away.

Janice kept her eyes locked on Rae. "You know, I think this is the first time I've even seen you in here."

A wave of panic washed over her, but Julian nodded solemnly and took her hand.

"We've only just taught her how to read."

"Was that really necessary?" Rae asked a few minutes later. She and Julian were huddled at a table in the corner, as far away from everyone else as they could get. "'Taught her how to read'?"

He nodded briskly and flipped another page. "Oh, I think so."

She rolled her eyes and leaned forward, keeping her own file open for good measure but keeping all her attention on his. "So...what does it say?"

He read softly under his breath, speaking so quietly that if anyone were to look it would appear that he was simply reading it to himself.

"Two people...an older couple...killed by a gunshot wound to the chest." He skimmed through, frowning slightly as he committed the page to memory. "Rae, it doesn't really say anything more in here than in the newspaper article you told me about. Only, instead of naming your dad as a suspect, they flat out list him as the perpetrator."

Rae's heart sank without her realizing it. She should have known better to hope. By now, she should have known better than to have even begun to hope...

"It says that?" she asked dully. "Just like that? That he did it?"

Julian gave her a quick look, but nodded sympathetically. "Yeah, it does. Says that while PC authorities were certain he had committed the crime they were forced to let him go, as there was nothing more than circumstantial evidence. It also says that agents Bethany Kerrigan and Jennifer Jones were sent to investigate the matter further."

Rae snorted in derision, more hurt than she was letting on. "Well, we all know how that part turned out, don't we? Happy endings all around."

Julian's face softened and he gave her shoulder a squeeze. "Hey...you okay? Were you, I don't know...were you really expecting to find anything different?"

Her eyes rested on the file and she sighed. "No. I wasn't."

He nodded gently and flipped it shut. "I just don't get it. Why did your dad want you to read this?" he mused. "It doesn't exactly exonerate him, and—"

All at once his body locked into place. His eyes flashed white as his hand simultaneously death-gripped the table beneath him. When he came to a second later, his face was pale. "*Shit*, Rae—"

But before he could explain, the door opened behind him and Rae saw what had him so spooked. With the look of someone who greatly enjoyed his work, Victor Mallins did a quick scan of the room, and then made a beeline right for them.

Jules! she shouted telepathically, palsied with fear.

"Stay cool," he breathed, making a visible effort to follow his own advice. "He's not after me, and I'm the one with the file. There's a chance he won't see..." As Mallins approached, he shifted his arm casually to cover up the names scribbled on the top of each case, turning in his chair to nod politely at the president. "Good afternoon, sir."

Mallins looked each one slowly up and down, seeming to relish the obvious tension radiating out of them. "Good afternoon, children. I see we're all hard at work today." His eyes raked across the table.

Rae leaned forward into his eye-line with a defiant smile. "Well you know me, sir. I like to keep busy." She knew his tatù, and this had nothing to do with it. He was up to something. Man, she couldn't stand that arrogant bastard.

He chuckled, a sound so splintered and chilling she thought for a moment that he and Janice might make a lovely pair. "Yes, you do. So what are we working on today?"

He glanced down at the file still open in front of Rae, and she flipped it up so he could see. "Just doing a little follow-up on our mark from last night. Jackman White. I took pictures of his files like you asked and gave them to President Carter last night."

Even hearing the name 'President Carter' seemed to grate on him, and she took in his discomfort with a satisfied smirk. On her other side, Julian kicked her warningly beneath the table.

"What about you, sir?" Julian continued respectfully. "It's not like the president of the Council to come down here and mix with us lowly agents." He tried for a smile, but was so wound up that it came out as more of a flinch.

Mallins smiled again. "Just stretching my legs. I was supposed to be sitting through another debriefing, but contrary to what you agents may think we supervisors really couldn't care less about your professional dramas."

These words had absolutely no effect whatsoever on Julian, but Rae was suddenly frozen to her chair. How was it possible that Victor Mallins had just used the exact same turn of phrase that both Luke and Molly had both said in their bedroom just an hour before?

You're being paranoid again, the little voice inside her head told her. *It's an extremely common expression. There's just...no other explanation.*

But looking at the wide grin stretching across Mallins' crooked face, Rae suddenly couldn't be so sure. Before she could lose her head entirely, he turned that grin to Julian.

"What about you, Julian? Working on anything interesting?"

It was only thanks to years of unabated friendship that Rae was able to guess what Julian was about to do next.

In what seemed like slow motion, he looked down to reach for the files. In the process, he sent them all 'accidently' spilling off the table with his elbow. Rae was quick to catch them, but in the process of handing them back, she held onto one file in particular, her grandparents', and simultaneously turned it invisible.

Julian reached out his hand and took them as if nothing at all unusual had just happened, holding them out for Mallins to see.

"Tresseux, Hilton, Funnel." He thumbed through them, looking almost bored. "Nothing all that interesting, to be honest. Just going back over a few details."

Mallins locked eyes on him, and for a moment Rae was worried the old man might take out a hidden weapon and blast her friend straight off the earth. But he didn't. He simply nodded once, and turned his attention back to her. "Miss Kerrigan, you're going to be training later this afternoon, yes?"

Rae hesitated, a little thrown off by the sudden change in gears. "Yeah, I'm actually headed there right after this." She glanced at Julian, not sure where this was going.

"Good. I have you paired up with Mr. Wardell." He met her look of dismay with a calm mask of indifference. "Should feel just like old times..."

"That's great." Rae forced herself to smile, despite feeling as though she might be sick. "Just great."

Rae walked into the PC training facility's gym an hour later, like a child venturing forth into the lion's den. She couldn't imagine a situation worse than the one she was about to encounter, and since Julian had stayed behind in the reference center to search for anything they might have missed, she was doing it completely alone.

She looked around uneasily as she crossed the empty, echoing floor. There was something weird about this. Something that went beyond her just not wanting to spar with Devon right after their tragic—

"Hey."

She jumped about a foot in the air, and came down clutching her chest. Then, with a look of scarcely concealed embarrassment, she turned slowly around.

Devon was walking slowly towards her, holding out something in his hand.

Her lips parted for the standard greeting, but just as she was about to speak a sudden chill ran up her arms.

My dream... This is exactly like my dream...

Once she recognized what it was that was setting her so on edge, it was impossible to shake it. It was as if the recurring nightmare had simply come to life; all the players and positions were the same. The only difference was that in place of a roaring crowd, the gym was dead quiet.

After one excruciating second, she decided she would have preferred the noise.

Devon walked towards her slowly, still holding out that same something in his hand. She almost forbade herself to look.

If it was a knife she was flat out bolting from the room, no questions asked.

"You okay?" he asked with a frown, automatically tensing up upon seeing her frozen expression. Before she could answer, he tossed something her way.

She almost shouted in relief when she caught it.

It was a water bottle. Not a knife. And her subconscious was officially driving her crazy. "Thanks," she smiled politely as she unscrewed the cap and took a swig. "Sorry, I just wasn't...I wasn't expecting to do this today."

His face clouded and he dropped his eyes to the floor. "Me neither. I mean, I was set up to train, but I thought..." His voice trailed off and she finished his sentence with a wry smile.

"You thought you'd be doing it without me."

All at once, the air between them was super-charged. His eyes hardened ever so slightly as he looked her up and down. Then, with a coldness she hardly ever saw from him, he lifted his chin and shook his head. "This wouldn't be my choice, no."

Her mouth started to fall open, but she caught herself sharply instead. *I can't believe he just said that. I can't believe he just looked me in the eyes and—*

"Shall we get started?" He headed to the wall where they kept the spears—his favorite weapon.

Without a word, she threw down the water bottle and headed there herself.

He wanted to fight it out? Fine, they would fight it out.

She wasn't too bad with a spear herself...

"I hope I didn't take you away from anything important," he began cryptically, touching the tip of his blade to hers to acknowledge and begin.

Without any preamble she took a mighty swing, causing him do duck almost to the floor if he didn't want to lose his head. "What would you have been interrupting?" she asked sweetly.

His eyes flashed and he pulled himself slowly to his feet. For a moment, neither of them moved. Then at the same time, they began slowly circling each other.

"I saw that you and Julian were in the reference center earlier," he explained. She took another swing at him and he blocked it so hard, the handle vibrated in her hand. "Didn't know that you two were planning on working there today."

Faster than the eye could see, she dropped down and whipped the spear in a wide arc towards his legs, knocking him backwards a step. "You saw us in the reference center? Well, you should have come over and said hi." She got to her feet, and marched towards him, spinning the weapon like a quick-moving propeller above her head. "Unless, of course, you didn't want us to see you there."

With the skill of a master, he planted his spear in the ground and used it to spin his body around through the air. He came at her feet first, kicking her squarely in the chest and knocking her onto her back. He landed beside her with a smug grin. "And why wouldn't I have wanted you to see me there?"

Throwing her spear aside she kicked him in the back of the knees, bringing him down to the floor beside her. "Maybe because you told Julian you were going to be somewhere else? Or maybe it was Luke this time." She tilted her head to the side, a glare on her face. "You've been telling so many lies lately, it must be hard to keep track."

He clenched his jaw and pushed away from her, getting to his feet in one fluid motion. She copied the movement behind him, ignoring it when he offered her a cursory hand up. "*I'm* the one telling lies?" he countered, tossing aside his spear as well so they could engage in hand-to-hand combat. "Tell me, Rae, what exactly were you and Julian doing in the reference center? And don't say catching up on old case files, because I know for a fact that you didn't even know we had a reference center until today."

With a cry of frustration, she flew towards him. He met her in the middle, and they both went crashing to the floor.

"Why can't you just talk to me?" she hissed between her teeth, straining to get the upper hand. At the last second, she was able to roll their bodies so that she was on top, straddling him.

"Like you talk to me?" He flipped them back around and came down on top of her, pinning her wrists to the mat above her head. "You're the one sneaking around."

"We're both sneaking around," she argued, trying and failing to free herself.

His eyes lit up in triumph. "So you admit it! You and Julian are up to something!"

She kneed him in the stomach and he rolled off of her with a groan.

"I admit nothing." Without another word, she started heading to the door. She didn't know exactly where this fight was going, but she certainly wasn't sticking around to find out.

She had made it almost all the way out, when she heard a sudden rush of air behind her. Her body tensed, and she turned around just in time for Devon to slam her up against the wall.

All the air rushed out of her body as she hit the plastic padding. Her body tried to crumble automatically forward, but Devon was right there, pressing his body against hers to keep it straight.

"We're not done sparring yet," he breathed, wrapping his fingers around her wrists and pressing them into the wall. His shoulders rose with quick, shallow breaths, and his muscles strained with the effort of keeping her there.

At first, her temper flared up and she wanted to scream at him. She wanted to push him away. She wanted to pry open that infuriating head and get at all the secrets there.

But as she stared into his eyes dilated with adrenaline, she found that she could do none of those things. All the strength and power seemed to rush from her body, and she heard herself speaking in a small, vulnerable voice. "Why did you kiss me?"

He took a step back at once. All the fight left him, as at the same time all the color seemed to drain right out of his face. He opened his mouth several times to speak, but nothing came out. "I just...I didn't..."

Rae held her breath, every fiber in her body aching for him to finish that sentence.

But he couldn't. He just ran his fingers back through his hair, and when his mask of composure finally crumbled, he was quick to turn his face away. "Sorry about the spears," he muttered and paced back across the gymnasium floor, leaving Rae standing there next to the far door, frozen in the exact place where he'd held her...

Silent tears streaming down her face.

A few hours later, Rae had collected herself and finally pushed open the door to the penthouse. After Devon had left her, she'd found herself suddenly unable to head home. Instead, she went through one of the tunnels that led to the Oratory and, finding it empty, she'd tossed up a rope and climbed to the top of the high domed ceiling, nestling in the wooden rafters like she used to.

Like *they* used to. When they used to talk and not just throw spears at each other.

Her purse dropped to the floor with a muted *thud* as she dragged her feet across the carpet to her room. It was only five or so in the afternoon, but she was ready for lights out.

Bed was a safe place. A place where nothing bad could happen to her, and this wretched, endless day couldn't possibly stretch out any further.

Her eyes closed wearily as she pushed open the door, ready to sink down into her amazing comforter and let the rest of the world just fall away—

"Finally, you're back!"

She leapt back against the door with a strangled shriek. Julian was sitting in the center of the bed, staring at her impassively. With a glare she peeled herself off the wall, taking off her jacket and throwing it with no real conviction towards her closet. Her tatùs were supposed to protect her from surprises. Why the hell was she always jumping around like a scared rabbit? *Probably because you're exhausted. And depressed. You have issues and your tatùs don't know what to do with you.* "If this is payback for this morning with you and Angel, you've terrible timing. As it's been made repeatedly clear to me today, I am, most definitely, single."

"It's not about that." For the first time, Rae noticed the sense of urgency in his voice. "Rae, I found something in the files..."

Chapter 12

"It's not what was in the files so much as...as where they were," Julian explained with a frown as Rae sat down beside him. "The other files that were with them."

She followed his troubled gaze down to his hands. There were smudges of ink all over them, hastily scribbled beneath the table. She picked one up and smoothed it out with concern.

"What is all this?" she asked softly, lifting it higher to read the writing. The dark lettering trailed out over his skin. "Or should I say...who are they?"

The names were seemingly endless, lacing from one end of his hand to the other. The ones at the top were larger, and easier to read. But the more he'd found the more distressed the script seemed to become—frantically trying to make them all fit.

"I don't..." He trailed off, shaking his head. "I don't know who—"

"*Hey*," Rae cut him off with alarm. She hadn't realized how upset he was, but the hand she still held in her own was suddenly shaking. She wrapped her arms around him without another thought, holding him tight until the trembling finally abated. When he had finally calmed down, she pulled back and searched his eyes carefully, trying to understand the emotion there. "What is it, Jules? What's wrong?"

He took a deep breath and tried started from the beginning. "I don't know who they are, because they weren't anywhere in the computer system. Not anything relevant at least." He shook his head with a weak smile. "Janice probably thinks I'm a freak; asking for people that aren't there. I guess it's probably for the best, though. If they didn't have files, then I couldn't be caught requesting their files..."

Rae shook her head. "Wait, I don't understand. If they didn't have files, then how did you even find out about them? How did you get these names?"

"When I went back to return your grandparents' papers, Janice asked me if I'd like to take a look at the others that had been filed along with it. Well, files are never 'filed together' in any sort of category, so I got curious and said yes. She gave me these names." He stared down at his hands once more, his dark eyes clouding over. "All that was there were the basics. Year of birth. Year they came to Guilder. Year they graduated. And then—nothing. So..." he finally lifted up his head, "I tried to see them."

It suddenly clicked. The reason he was feeling this so personally. The emotions that had shaken him to the core.

Rae closed her eyes and rubbed him gently on the back. "Of course you did."

"But I couldn't." The words flew out of him now, fast and confused. And afraid. "After reading the files, I knew their age. Their stories. I saw their pictures and had their faces floating in my mind." He turned to Rae slowly and carefully enunciated each word. "There is simply no reason why I wouldn't be able to see where they are now. Or what happened to them. It's like...it's like they all just disappeared."

Something in the words jogged Rae's memory, and she looked up in horror.

"Or...they *were* disappeared."

Julian's eyes locked with hers and both of them grew suddenly still.

They had both been there that night in Texas, when their new friend Camille's parents had explained why it was they had kept her on the run. People with tatùs that exceeded a certain limit on the Privy Council's 'risk-o-meter' often vanished and were never heard from again. It was the reason they had taken their daughter to start a new life off the grid. It was the same reason that every other person they'd met was on the run from the Privy Council.

Rae thought back to the words of her father.

"...I would ask you to take a closer look at the workings of the high and mighty Privy Council. They were not always as spotless and forthcoming as they would have people think. You need proof? Just ask Pete and Kathy..."

He knew she would find this. He knew she would go to see their file, only to end up finding all the other Privy Council cold cases... All the other people who vanished without a trace. She sucked in a sharp breath, horrified at the realization.

"You can't think..." Julian looked a little sick. "You can't actually think the Council had a hand in this."

"The Council had me arrested. The Council hid for years behind the 'certainty' that a man they needed to believe was dead wasn't wreaking havoc and infiltrating their organization. The Council dictated impossible laws about how we can live, and who we can love...and put countless families on the run because the parents wanted to protect their *children*." She took a slow, deep breath to steady herself. "Yeah, Julian. I can believe the Council is capable of pretty much anything."

Julian was shaking his head, his mind rebelling against the idea. Unlike Rae, he had grown up in the tatù society. Until his missing father had returned, they had been his only anchor of support. The possibility that their leading body, the Privy Council, could be no better than their enemies... He couldn't believe it to be so. He wouldn't.

"Rae, please," he pleaded softly, "think about what you're saying. I mean...we *work* for these people. They basically raised us. You really think they could—"

She took his hand again, pressing her finger into each of the names. "Think about it, Jules. Churches have killed in the name of salvation, kingdoms have destroyed in the name of freedom or more land. What makes you think the Privy Council didn't get greedy at one point? Look what everyone is doing to the earth. Shouldn't it be treated as sacred?" She wanted to cry. "It makes sense. What about that book of ink in the Guilder library? It lists every tatù that's ever been born in order of category, right? Some are common, some are rare; it goes up in levels, right?"

He nodded reluctantly and tried to pull his hand away, but she wouldn't let go.

"Julian, in all your years here have you ever seen one of the rare tatùs walking around?" *Besides me?* she added silently, wondering if the only reason she was still here was because of her father.

It was like a light went out inside of Julian. His shoulders fell and his body flinched like he was expecting to get hit. It was true. She'd just convinced him.

But then, just as suddenly, a light went on as well.

He looked up at her with rigid intensity, staring deep into her eyes. "Just you."

As obvious as it was, it was a piece she hadn't quite put together yet, and hearing it said aloud sent chills careening up and down her arms. What did that mean? Were her days here numbered as well? But just as she considered it, she realized that it also wasn't entirely true.

"And Ellie," she added, thinking of her young friend.

The names strung together as easily as could be, bringing along with them a natural truth.

Julian's voice was as low and fractured as she'd ever heard it. "You think the Council is imprisoning hybrids." He didn't say it as a question. They knew by now it was a fact. "To kill them or to...to experiment on them?"

They both thought back to Cromfield's dungeon, and automatic tears filled their eyes.

"What does it matter?" Rae answered. Her voice was cold, not an ounce of emotion left to give it any color. "Who the hell is going to know...if they've simply disappeared?" She suddenly wanted to disappear as well.

Rae went out walking alone that night. She had been grateful for Julian's company at the time, but after coming to terms with what had happened both of them needed to be alone. He went back to his house to pick up Angel for a long drive, and Rae wandered the darkened London streets.

The Privy Council imprisoned hybrids. Vanished them because they were too dangerous to control.

She turned the words over and over again in her head, trying to accustom herself to the horrifying reality. Strangely enough, it wasn't the words themselves that were hard to believe. It was the fact that it had been happening right under her nose this whole time.

And right in front of who else? She couldn't help but ask the question.

Did Jennifer know? Lanford? Did Dean Wardell know what was going on? Did Rogers or Callam—her old case commanders? Did Carter know what the Council had done? Was possibly still doing?

She forced herself to answer no to these last two questions. Carter could not have known what was happening; she refused to believe he could. She also refused to believe it was possible that these sort of mass abductions were still going on.

With the school sitting on top of the Council rooms? Guilder students walking around on the grass right above the holding cells? It was too much. Someone would have seen something, would have reported something. Someone would have had a friend go missing, and then the cat would be out of the bag.

No, this had to have happened years ago, in the dead of night. Most likely during the Simon Kerrigan Scandal, she realized with an ironic start. When someone else was already front page, ready to take all the blame...

She had wandered in a wide circle, around the river and back to her home. She was just passing the garden now, breathing in the beautiful orchids as she walked past Julian and Devon's new house. She was halfway past it and heading back to her apartment, when she noticed the strange town car pulling to a stop in front of their driveway.

Acting on instinct, she ducked quickly behind a clump of bushes and watched with narrowed eyes. The driver's door opened, and she held her breath. But out stepped the last man in the world she expected to see.

Wasn't that...wasn't that the old man they'd met in San Francisco? The chemist from Oxford?

Rae watched in amazement as he darted around the back of the car and pulled open the front passenger door. What she saw next amazed her even more.

Devon tried once to step out onto the curb, but gave up almost immediately and fell back against his seat. It wasn't until the elderly professor took his arm that he was able to manage it, leaning heavily on the old man all the while. The two of them hobbled up the front steps, at which point the man turned to Devon and began speaking in an urgent undertone. Even using the fox tatù, Rae was unable to make out what they were saying. But whatever it was, Devon wasn't having it. He simply raised a shaky hand, and shook his head. He thanked the man kindly for whatever it was that had happened, and turned to the door. After fumbling around in the lock for a few seconds he finally got his key to work, and disappeared inside. The old man stared after him for a long while, before eventually returning to his car and driving off into the night.

Rae couldn't think. She could only react.

Devon was inside that house alone. And he was hurting.

In a flash of speed, she bolted up the front steps, throwing open and front door and slamming it shut again behind her. "Devon?" she called as she paced hurriedly through the house, searching for him. "Devon, where are you?"

She found him at the base of the stairs. His back was to her with one hand gripping the banister, but he had frozen in place when he heard her voice.

"Listen—enough games, okay? You need to tell me what the hell is going—"

Then he collapsed.

"DEVON?!"

All her anger vanished in a heartbeat as she raced over to catch him before he could hit the ground. As she turned him gently over onto her lap, she sucked in a quick breath of air. He looked terrible. His tan skin was a sickly ashen color, his legs and arms twitched with periodic spasms, and there were dark sinister-looking bruises beneath his red-rimmed eyes.

"Rae?" His eyes flitted open and he looked incredibly confused to see her there. "What are you...what you doing here?"

"What are *you* doing?!" she shot back, her voice shrill with panic. "Why the hell are you on the ground—what happened?!" Her heart raced, her body flipping through tatùs, trying to find one to fix the problem that she felt helpless to stop.

He tried to push up onto his arms, without any luck. "Just go. I'm fine."

"Bullshit you're fine! You just collapsed."

Holding him steady with one hand, she pulled out her phone with the other and began pressing buttons at the speed of light. The fact that she could restrain him with one hand absolutely terrified her, and she dialed even faster.

"Don't," he breathed, still trying to get up, "don't call anyone. Please."

She ignored him and held it up to her ear. There was flood of background noise as the line clicked open, and then a young woman's voice answered cheerfully on the other end. "Hello?"

"Alicia?"

"Rae?" she sounded surprised. "Hey! Haven't heard from you in a while; what's going on? Is everything okay?"

Rae's eyes travelled over Devon, and her face paled. "No, everything's not okay. I'm going to text you an address. Can you come over here, please? It's an emergency."

There was a brief pause.

"I'll be right there."

The line went dead.

One of the good things about growing up in a tightknit group of tatùs, isolated from the rest of the world, was that it made you family. When someone asked you to come—you came.

"It's okay, honey," she murmured, stroking a hand across Devon's scalp, "Alicia's on her way. The hospital is only a few minutes from here and..." She trailed off, watching him in horror.

He had flinched away from her touch, rubbing his temples like he was on some kind of sensory overload. She tried again to soothe him, but he recoiled even further.

"Please, don't touch me," he groaned, looking at her like she was the worst thing that could have possibly walked through his door. "Just—" she raised her hand again, and he slapped it out of the air, "get away from me!"

She dropped her arms to her sides, feeling as though he'd just hit her with his car. Still cringing on the ground, Devon looked up in horror.

"I didn't mean it like that," he gasped, clutching his hair in fists and shaking like a leaf in the wind. "I'm sorry, I didn't—." He fell back with a groan, squeezing his eyes shut; curling up so his knees were pressed against his forehead.

Rae had no idea what to do. Over the years she'd seen him hurt. She'd seen him damaged. Hell, she'd seen him almost dying.

But she'd always known what had caused it. She'd always known, in theory, how to fix it. This was something else entirely.

As tentatively as possible and instinctively taking care to avoid his skin, she picked him up and half-carried him to the sofa. She was just helping him lie down when there was a knock on the door and Alicia rushed inside.

"Good thing you called when you did," she exclaimed, taking off her jacket and setting her bag down on the floor. "I was out at a restaurant just around the corner—"

She stopped cold when she saw Devon, and her face grew abruptly grave. "What happened?"

Devon leaned back against the cushions, unable to speak, and Rae simply shook her head with tears in her eyes. "I don't know!" she cried. "He won't tell me!"

For a split second all was still.

Then, like flipping a switch, Alicia turned into 'doctor mode.'

Rae took a step back and watched with the only flicker of hope she'd felt since seeing Julian's hands a few hours before. Aside from Ellie's hybridism and Julian's unprecedented clairvoyance, Alicia's was the only tatù she had been unable to master. She suspected it was due to the complex nature of the ink. Alicia was a diagnostician. In fact, she was the best diagnostician in the world. There was no one on the planet Rae would rather have looking at Devon right now.

Already she had sunk to her knees in front of the sofa, and was running her hands gently up and down his body. Rae watched in terror as her lovely face clouded. "What is it?" she asked pre-emptively. "What's wrong?"

Even Devon was staring up fearfully, waiting for Alicia's response.

"It's...everything," she murmured. "Your whole body... it's in some kind of shock." Her face tilted to the side as her brow furrowed in concentration. "I'm not sure quite what to—"

All at once, she jumped back like something had startled her. Her head snapped up and she stared at Devon in amazement. Devon on the other hand stared back without surprise... almost as if he had been waiting for it to happen. Almost as if he had planned it.

For a second, they were lost in their own private communication. Then Alicia pushed slowly to her feet. As Rae looked on in wonder, Alicia glanced between the two of them and shook her head.

"This is...I'm going to leave this to the two of you."

She'd already put on her coat and picked up her bag, when Rae snapped back into action.

"What?!" she cried, grabbing Alicia by the arm and steering her back to Devon. "What're you talking about? He's sick, Aly! Look at him! There's something—"

"I told you already," she answered quietly, reclaiming her arm, "he's in shock. I don't know what caused it, but I do know it's no longer life-threatening. He needs to rest." She moved back towards the door, but squeezed Rae's hand on her way out. "Rae—I can't stay here for this."

Then she was gone.

Rae and Devon stared at each other for a brief moment after the door closed.

Then there was an explosion.

"What the HELL is going on here?!" Rae shouted, towering over the couch.

He pushed himself up as best he could, matching her in volume and rage. "You don't have a right to know. Just drop it!"

"Yes, I do!" she cried, eyes welling up with tears. "Damn it Devon! You're my best friend in the whole world. I love you. I need you! You have to tell me what happened—"

"I don't have to tell you anything," he interrupted. "I'll be fine. Just get out of here. I need to sleep."

It was the strangest thing. She sensed that he didn't want to hurt her—that it was literally killing him to say these things—but yet, here he was doing it anyway; causing just enough damage that she would be offended and leave. Well, she wasn't one to be shaken off so easily.

"Devon, please. I just want to help—"

"WE'RE BROKEN UP!" he shouted, raising himself up on his elbows and staring her down. "We don't kiss under beds anymore; we don't hold hands. You CHEATED on me! We're not together anymore and it's YOUR FAULT!"

A sob shook through her body as a dozen tears spilled over her face. Without thinking about it, she reached out and took his hand. But as soon as she touched him, he wheeled back in pain.

"Don't—" he began, but something distracted him.

They both looked down at her hand. Then down at his.

There was a huge red mark where her fingers had been just seconds before. Like she had burned him. Her breath caught in her throat, and when she spoke her voice was rough and low. "Devon...what did you do?"

He was shaking. All over, he was shuddering. But when he spoke, he had never been so sure.

"Rae...get the hell out of my house."

Chapter 13

Rae ran out of Devon's house like a bat out of hell.

She didn't bother to hide her speed from any late-night voyeurs who might be watching. She didn't do a thing to stop the constant stream of tears either, nor did she even bother to take the time to stop and think. By all accounts, she might have continued running for hours if a familiar humming in her skin hadn't stopped her dead in her tracks.

She broke out of the run and came to a standstill so abrupt that the path ahead of her was showered with a spray of dirt and broken bits of stone. Her sharp breath echoed in the still night and she held her hands out in front of her.

It was Devon's tatù. Her eyes narrowed as she suddenly realized what was throwing her off her game. It was Devon's tatù and she couldn't stand to be using it a second longer.

Without stopping to think, she switched to something else. Anything else. Anything that wasn't a part of her vengeful ex-boyfriend.

Her brow furrowed as a rather unfamiliar feeling floating to the surface. It was something she recognized, yes, but not something she was in any way accustomed to.

Julian.

His name popped into her head as she simultaneously identified his tatù. She supposed it made sense that she would have slipped into his, as ill-equipped as she was. In times like this, her body instinctively chose the ink that would most serve to protect her.

And right now, she couldn't think of anything she needed more.

She whipped out her phone and was about to the press speed dial, when she suddenly paused. How could she answer his questions when she had no idea what was going on? How could she even string together a coherent sentence right now? A flashback of Devon's furious screams echoed through her head, and she shuddered.

There was no way in heaven or hell she would leave him alone in this. Even now. Even after how many times he'd told her to leave.

But there was no way she was steady enough to handle it either.

In the end, she texted Julian a simple *Devon SOS* and started walking slowly back her penthouse.

Molly and Luke were either holed up together or out for the night. Either way the door was closed. Rae welcomed the isolation. There was truly nothing and nobody who could comfort her right now. A line had been crossed. A bridge had been broken. And while she and Devon may have been on a temporary break before, it certainly didn't feel so temporary now.

She sat down in the middle of her bed and stared blankly at the wall.

It wasn't that he had shouted something in pain and anger. That, she understood. And she would never hold him accountable for words said in distress.

It was that everything he shouted was the truth.

Whatever had happened to him tonight, it had stripped away some of the inhibitions and emotional barriers that had kept him quiet for so long. Like a truth serum, a flood of honesty had poured out, stripping her bare. Stripping the bond between them.

It was over. Her heart wanted to break.

There was a sudden rustle of paper, and she looked down in surprise to see that she had conjured a pen and notepad. The second she had, her body switched back to Julian's tatù.

Well...her mind may know that it was over. However, her body would need a bit more convincing.

Indulging herself this one last time, she focused all the energy she could on seeing what was happening right now in the house across the park. Unlike Julian, she couldn't just white out her eyes and see it in a vision. She was back where he had been when they first met at Guilder, scribbling half-formed versions of the future down with paper and ink.

And unlike Julian, Rae most certainly did not possess a natural artistic flare.

She looked down when she was finished, and almost laughed out loud at the parade of stick figures marching out in front of her. There was someone who looked kind of like Julian—at least he had a ponytail—and someone who looked kind of like Angel, with a sheet of long white hair. Julian was turning the car around in a sharp U-turn. She knew that, because she had also unconsciously doodled the word 'U-turn', and from the jagged buildings in the background, it looked like they were flying back to London.

Well, it may have lacked Julian's finesse but she got the general idea. In fact, a small part of her thought she may have it framed and sent to his house. He would be proud. At the very least, it would give him a much-deserved laugh.

Reduced to a coil of raw nerves with time to kill, Rae tried again, her hand flying over the page as she tracked their progress.

By now they were at the house. Julian was kneeling in front of the sofa, looking as terrified as Rae's two-dimensional drawing would allow, while Angel paced in the background, holding what looked to be a phone. As for Devon...? Rae couldn't tell if he was sleeping or passed out. His eyes were closed, that much was clear, but she wasn't able to get much of anything else from it.

Frustrated, she ripped off the top sheet of paper she was working on and started anew.

This time, her hand never stopped moving as it flew across the page. She could tell that she was probably getting ink all over her comforter, but she kept up her speed—reaching out with her mind and willing herself to see more. When she finally finished, she looked down eagerly to see what she had come up with. Only...what she saw didn't make any sense.

Gone where her characters. Gone was the house.

She held the paper closer to her face and squinted with a frown as she tried to decipher it. It was a rather simple drawing. A closed door with a hand reaching for the knob. In fact...she twisted it around to get a better angle...if she didn't know any better, she would swear it was—

"Well, this is some really talented stuff."

She dropped the paper on the bed and looked up to see Gabriel thumbing through her previous drawings. Her senses had become so caught up in Julian's tatù that she hadn't heard anyone come inside.

"When did you get here?!" she demanded, trying to snatch them back with no success.

"Sometime while you were trying and failing to be a psychic." He tilted one of them to the side and cocked his head. "This— for example. It looks like Julian fell down, Devon passed out, and Angel...? My best bet is that Angel's in the background, ordering a pizza."

"Give me that!" She grabbed it out of his hand and stuffed it childishly below her pillow. "It isn't nice to sneak up on people, you know. Or didn't your demented father-figure teach you that in the cave?"

He sank onto the bed with a sarcastic grin. "You know why that's funny? Because I was *actually* kidnapped as a child and forced to work as a slave."

"Don't try to make me feel sorry for you." She turned her head with a sniff. "You're the one who came creeping in here."

"It wasn't exactly a sneak attack, Rae. I knocked, then came in."

"Well, I was..." she glanced down helplessly at her empty pad of paper, "...distracted."

He smiled at her fondly. "Yes, you were." Without another word, he stripped off his jacket and shoes and lay back against the pillows, making himself more comfortable. "So, do you want to tell me what's going on? Or should we just skip all that and jump right into bed?"

"I think the Privy Council did exactly what Cromfield's been doing." Rae hadn't expected to say it. Especially not to Gabriel. But there it was, right out in the open. She continued on in the same inflectionless monotone. "I think they took hybrids by force and locked them away somewhere." Her eyes grew hard as stone. "Because it's the *hybrids* who are dangerous."

She looked back up to see Gabriel watching her impassively.

It was the worst thing he could have done.

He could have shaken his head, looked horrified. He could have sworn up and down that he had been there while Cromfield was doing the same thing, and then told Rae to trust him, none of the signs were matching up.

But he did none of those things. In fact, he looked remarkably unsurprised.

"Anyone you know in particular?" he asked.

She lifted her head. "No, but what does that matter? It happened. It happened to a hell of a lot of people, and there are still hybrids out there on the run. Something has to be done. Someone has to be held accountable."

Perhaps it was the result of living in abject, nightmarish hell for so long, but no matter the circumstance Gabriel had an uncanny ability of staying bright and above it all. Even now, he was staring at her with a sparkle in his eyes. Looking almost...proud. "So what're you going to do about it?"

Her heart sank an inch lower in her chest, and she bowed her head in defeat. The words sealed the deal. Now, more than ever, she knew it had to be true. "What would you do?" she asked quietly, praying for some kind of inspiration.

"Get proof. Tell Carter."

Her head snapped up again and she stared at him in silence. They may joke about it now, but the years growing up in the catacombs had also made him unshakably pragmatic.

Of course! In this twisted, tangled mess of a situation—that was the obvious answer.

Get proof. Tell Carter.

"That's what you would do?" she repeated, head swirling with the beginnings of a plan.

He threw back his head with a sparkling laugh. "No. *I* would leave it alone. I would forget all about it, take off your clothes, and finally consummate this unholy love of ours." He met her dumbfounded look with a cheerful shrug. "But we've always had different priorities."

She shook her head with a soft chuckle. Angel and Gabriel were some of the most deeply disturbed people she had ever met. But sometimes there was no one better to have around.

"So you'd tell *Carter*?" She looked at him carefully, asking the silent question and waiting on pins and needles for his response.

His face sobered instantly and he gazed back with a serious nod. "Yeah, I would."

Thank the Maker! They were on exactly the same page. There was no way Carter could be a part of this.

She nodded thoughtfully then flashed him a quick grin, trying to lighten the mood. "Well, given your history with the man, that's actually rather brave of you."

He smiled, though his eyes remained thoughtful. "Carter may not trust me anymore, but I still trust him. I'd trust him with my life."

The words hung heavy in between them as both of them weighed the chilling consequence of what would happen if they were wrong.

"With your *life?*" she finally joked.

He flashed her a grin. "Well, I'd at least have some sort of a back-up plan..."

Gabriel left shortly after. He didn't ask what else was bugging Rae, and she appreciated his non-prying nature. He kept her thoughts distracted from Devon. She had no idea what had happened to Devon, but whatever it was, he no longer wanted her to be a part of it. The sooner she accepted it, the better. Their last kiss... well, it must have been a sad good-bye.

Growing up was hard. Heartbreak sucked big time.

She didn't sleep well that night. Although there were hundreds of new things to fret about, she kept tossing and turning with the same recurring dream...

It was exactly as it had been before, only everything was happening much faster now.

She was standing in the center of the Oratory floor, and Devon had just handed her a knife.

He made his usual denials, and she called out to him as he turned and walked away. But by now, she didn't expect him to stay. Already her eyes were on the fog at the other end of the room, waiting for her father.

Simon Kerrigan walked slowly forward, appearing from the exact spot where Devon had vanished just seconds earlier. He was holding the same blade as she was, and she took a step back as he unsheathed it.

But scared as she may be, she understood there was nothing to fear. At least, not from him.

"Dad?"

She was speeding things up this time. Trying to find the perpetrator. Trying to jump ahead to identify the man still lurking in the shadows.

"Dad, you have to help me," she said, deviating from the script. "He's coming, and I don't—"

But just then, Simon's eyes fixed on something behind her and she knew it was too late. "Rae—look out!"

Her body whirled around just as the silver blade flew into her stomach. There was a muffled screaming coming from somewhere above her, but she couldn't lift her up eyes to see. She couldn't tear them away from the man standing in front of her—slowly lifting off his dark hood...

"Rae!"

Her eyes opened with a gasp and she sat up in alarm, still clutching at her stomach. Julian was sitting on the bed in front of her, gazing down with concern.

"Geez, hon...are you okay?"

She shook her head back and forth. She knew her eyes were as wide as saucers. "There's a bug!"

He raised his eyebrows but remained calm, glancing around at her tangled sheets. "There was a bug in your dream, or you saw something—?"

"In the house, Julian!" she interrupted. "There's a surveillance bug in our house!"

A second later, she was a blur of color. Dressing, searching, and generally racing through the different rooms as Julian followed behind her, trying to keep up.

"Hang on." He lifted his hands pragmatically. "Why the hell do you think there's a—"

"Think about it." She stopped dead in her tracks and whirled about, gesturing to the living room around her. "How did Mallins know I would be at your house that morning when he came to pick me up? How did he know that you and I were both heading to the library?" She continued her frantic search—

overturning vases and tearing pictures off the wall. "How the hell was it that he used the exact same phrase in the afternoon that both Molly and Luke had said that morning? It makes no sense! He has to have a bug in here!"

Julian trailed behind, but looked doubtful. "Rae, do you have any idea how difficult it is to get approval for a PC listening device? How many privacy laws it obstructs? Laws that were created by the *same* Council you think put one here?"

"Yeah, but it wouldn't be that hard for the president himself to order one, would it?"

He bit his lip and glanced nervously around. "No, I suppose not..."

After another fruitless search, Rae came to stop in the middle of the carpet. There had to be something she could do to speed this up. Someone weapon in her arsenal she had yet to employ.

Closing her eyes in concentration, she took a mental step back and let her body take control, giving it free rein to choose whatever would help her most.

What it ended up choosing surprised her.

Gabriel's tatù?

It buzzed—loud and eager through her skin—and she frowned as she considered it. She'd only used it once or twice before, and while the premise was clear the actual mechanics eluded her.

In a bit of a Hail Mary, she held out her open palm and spoke in a commanding voice.

"Come!"

Nothing happened.

To Julian's credit, he wasn't openly laughing. But he was looking at her as though worried that she may have actually lost her mind.

"Rae, what are you—"

"COME!"

He leaned back against the counter and folded his arms. "Kerrigan, be serious. Do you honestly think there's any chance in hell that's going to work?"

A tiny metallic disk flew into her outstretched hand.

Julian's mouth fell open as she examined it carefully. While Devon had been the one to put a similar device on Jackman White, she was fairly certain this was the same kind of thing. In fact, when she held it close enough and squinted, she could just barely make out the Council seal.

Her lips curled up in a smirk as she tossed it Julian's way.

"Still think the Council wouldn't bug our homes?"

His face paled, but he didn't deny it. In fact, as he crushed it between his fingers he could say only one word. "*Angel.*"

As it turned out, Julian and Rae went jogging together after all.

Running was more like it.

The two of them tore through the park without restraint, bolting towards his house. As great as the intrusion was, Rae didn't see any particular time crunch to destroy it now. Why not misdirect a little? But as Julian pointed out, if Mallins was listening on the other end then he already knew they'd found one device. It was only a matter of time before he retaliated, and there was no telling what that retaliation might be...or how many people might get involved.

They went tearing into the front room just as Angel was wandering down the stairs, still wearing a tiny pair of pajamas. Her eyes widened in surprise when she saw them.

"Hey, babe, I thought you were headed over to Rae's house to talk about Dev—"

Julian lifted a finger to his lips, and glanced warily around the house—as if the listening devices might just be cameras as well.

When he was satisfied that no one was about to bust in the door, he turned to Rae expectantly.

"Do it."

Feeling particularly grim, Rae lifted her hand as she done before and called out for the devices, latching onto any metal signature in the room she could find. No fewer than three shiny disks flew into her hand.

The three teenagers stared down at them like one might peer at a bomb, waiting at any moment for the delayed explosion.

Then with a burst of fury Rae rarely saw, Julian crushed them to a pulp in his fist.

"I don't understand..." Angel's face was pale. "Was that—?"

Julian turned to Rae. "Do the rest of the rooms," he asked softly. "Please."

She nodded and headed up the stairs, while he turned back and began quietly explaining what was going on to Angel. There was another device in the upstairs hallway, and two more in the loft. She found a single disk lodged inside a wooden bookshelf in their shared bedroom, but for the sake of preserving their sanity, she kept that one to herself.

Twice as she passed by Devon's closed door, she considered knocking. In fact, she considered opening it up and barging on in, demanding an explanation for the previous night.

But again reason ruled out over emotion, and she headed back downstairs. They had a much more immediate problem than a failed romance to deal with right now.

The second he saw her Julian raced over, meeting her at the bottom of the stairs. "Did you find anything else?"

She nodded. "Three more," she handed them over and gave him the honors, "one in the hallway and two in the loft."

He crushed them mercilessly against the banister, taking a grim sort of pleasure in it before turning to her with worried eyes. "There wasn't...you didn't find any inside the—"

"Just the hallway and loft," she repeated, keeping the rest to herself.

He nodded swiftly and held up his phone. "I texted Molly and told her to come over right away. There's just no way we can keep this to ourselves anymore. It's bigger than that."

She nodded in agreement and sank down onto the couch next to Angel. It most certainly was. Half of her was surprised the PC cavalry hadn't busted in already. Half of her was wondering if she should be calling Carter.

"I still don't get it," Angel said in a low voice. The bugs might have been officially destroyed, but the fear of them remained. "When exactly did they break in and do this? These things had to have already been in the house before you and Julian even got back from the airport."

"Mallins has always suspected me," Rae shook her head with a sigh, "from the moment I broke into the PC to steal the piece of my father's device. He never accepted the fact that I was doing it to protect them. Even when I gave it back, he's always thought I had ulterior motives."

Angel nodded quietly, watching Julian pace back and forth with her wide, sapphire eyes.

"I'm amazed he hasn't asked me to leave yet," she muttered. "The Council has to know by now who I am, and if there's a chance they might be coming. I'm amazed he hasn't told me to run for the hills."

"Would you?"

"No, but that's never stopped him before."

Rae had to admire her pluck. "The Council has apparently known who you are for a long time," she assured her, stringing two and two together even as she spoke. "They could have come at any time, but didn't. Mallins has some other reason for doing this. One that doesn't have anything to do with you."

Angel pursed her lips, but continued to watch Julian with a worried frown. "Let's hope."

Let's hope...

The words struck Rae as almost funny. Because they'd been having such great luck lately, right? With another sigh she dropped her head into her hands, wishing Molly would hurry up.

What the hell were they supposed to do? Was another Council confrontation on the way?

She was hyper-aware of the fact that the entire hybrid-exposing conversation she and Julian had the night before had been right there in her bedroom. Granted, she hadn't found any disks in there, but who knows how much just one of them could pick up?

"Rae?"

She glanced over and saw Angel looking at her with concern. She paused for a moment, then, in a most uncharacteristic move, she actually reached out and squeezed Rae's hand.

"Devon's alright, by the way. We stayed with him until he was able to walk up the stairs on his own. Jules also called your friend Alicia about twelve more times, and she swore up and down he'd be fine. He even went out this morning to the gym."

To the gym. Yeah, sure.

But still, the icy fist gripping Rae's heart relaxed a fraction of an inch. "That's...that's really good to hear. Thanks, Angel."

"Sure."

She would have liked to grill her further, but at that very moment Molly burst through the door—Luke hot on her heels. "Guys! We need to talk!"

Julian threw up his hands. "Yeah, we do! You won't believe what Rae and I found this—"

"It can wait," Molly interrupted him, looking pale. She turned to Luke and gestured him forward. "Tell them, babe. Tell them exactly what you just told me."

Luke stepped into the middle of the room, looking extremely uncomfortable as he glanced around at their tightknit circle. "I was at the office this morning, going over some intercepted communications, and..." He faltered. "Now, keep in mind, I could be drawn and quartered just for telling you this, but—"

Molly stamped her foot. "Babe, there's no time!"

He sighed and dropped his eyes to the floor. "They're going to arrest you, Rae."

It was like someone had poured a glass of icy water down her spine. She stiffened automatically, every muscle in her body on high alert as she got slowly to her feet. "Who is?"

Luke's face tightened. "Your own people. The Privy Council. Victor Mallins put out the order about twenty minutes ago. I think they're gearing up for it right now..."

Molly raced forward and took her hand, while Julian stepped protectively in front of her.

"And what exactly are they arresting her for?" he demanded. "If it has anything to do with those files, we were perfectly within our right to—"

"No, it wasn't anything about files," Luke interrupted. "Apparently, she's been officially labeled as too great a risk. Something about having 'dangerous potential'..."

In spite of the gravity of the situation, Rae's lips turned up in a hard smile. "Then it looks like you got it wrong, Luke. I'm not being arrested."

Her eyes locked with Julian's.

"I'm being disappeared."

Chapter 14

It was like looking down in a dream, only to realize the floor you were standing on had suddenly disappeared. In this town, in this lifetime, things could change just that quickly.

Julian, Molly, Luke, and Angel circled around Rae in a bizarre kind of orbit. Each a blur of movement, each throwing out suggestions. Each keeping their eyes simultaneously on the door.

"Rae! You've got to call Carter!" Angel commanded. Within a second, Luke had seconded the idea.

While, ironically, they were the only two people in the room not to have any personal loyalty to the man, based on his reputation alone they were willing to trust him.

"Carter will know what to do," Luke continued. "He can put a stop to this!"

"Julian!" Molly demanded, her voice shrill. "What do you see?"

Julian paused a minute in his rotation, his eyes glassing over to iridescent white. Rae glanced at him quietly, watching while Angel rushed forward to give him a steadying hand, but she didn't need to see his reaction to know that the news wasn't good.

"There isn't..." He bowed his head, brow furrowing in concentration as he tried even harder, but it was to no avail. "No decision has been made. Everyone's just been given orders." His eyes cleared and focused on Rae. "Luke's right. It's orders to come here."

"*Call Carter*," Angel said again, tossing her hair back as she simultaneously kept an eye on both the front and back door.

Julian shook his head. "We can call him, sure, but whatever Mallins put in motion is already too late to reverse. By the time he gets to Rae, she'll be..." His voice trailed off as she shot her a panicked look. "Call him anyway," he instructed Luke. "Tell him who you are and tell him to get here immediately."

Luke nodded and whipped out his phone, getting the number from Molly.

"I'm calling Gabriel," Angel murmured, pulling out her own phone. "If this thing's about to go flying off the rails, there's no way I'm leaving without him..."

Molly's enormous eyes locked on Rae in fear. "Maybe you should call your mom. Beth would know what to do. She could think of a way to hide you, or appeal to the PC or something..."

At the same time, Julian stepped suddenly forward and took Rae's hand. "Rae, you're not going to like it, but you need to call Devon. If you don't, then I will. I don't care what sort of weird fight you two are in. If he knew what was going on here, he would—"

"He would come charging straight in here to rescue me," Rae cut him off. "And end up getting hurt, or fired, or arrested right alongside me." The room fell silent when Rae finally spoke. Her chest rose up and down with quick, shallow breaths, but when she spoke again, her voice was soft and sure. "Call Carter, call my mom, call whomever you like," she breathed. "But no one, *do you hear me*, NO ONE is calling Devon. This is the *exact* reason I wanted to keep him out of this." Her eyes travelled around the circle. "This is the *exact* reason I wanted to keep all of you out of this."

Julian shot her a look of strained patience, but finally nodded his head. "Fine. Whatever. He can come and meet up with us once we find a place. Molly, why don't you start making travel arrangements? Afterwards, you can call Beth. Angel, if you want Gabriel to come along then get him here right now. We don't know the next time we'll be in London. And Luke—"

"Hang on!" Rae held up a hand, halting the sudden flurry of movement. "What exactly are you talking about?"

Julian and Molly shared a quick glance, before she said, "Rae, we've got to get you out of here. If you think that we're going to let you get arrested by the Privy Council again, then you're out of your—"

"I'm not running."

The room stopped cold, all eyes turning towards her at once. Angel even lowered the phone away from her ear, ignoring Gabriel shouting something on the other end.

Julian glanced at Molly again, before stepping forward. "Rae, I know you're freaked out right now, but this is when we need to pull together. If we don't get you out, Mallins and the PC will throw you into a black hole somewhere, and no matter how hard we try to find you, we won't—"

"If I run now, that's the ballgame." She met his look of panic with an even stare. "I'll be running for the rest of my life. My freakin' ETERNAL life. And I can kiss goodbye any sort of life I wanted to have here." An image of Devon's face flashed through her mind. "Any sort of future..." She pulled herself together and straightened up to her full height. "That's not something I'm willing to do."

Molly glanced again at the front door, tapping her foot nervously. "So, what precisely do you suggest?"

Rae's breath caught in her chest as she stared around the room. Four beautiful faces stared back at her. Four of her closest friends in the whole world, ready to march with her into the fire.

Only...she couldn't let them.

"This isn't something I can let you do," she murmured, almost to herself. "This isn't something I can let you risk."

No one here had Devon's super hearing, so they all looked at her curiously, unable to make out what she had said.

"Sorry, Rae," Molly began, taking a step forward, "what?"

Rae met her eyes and gave her a sad smile. "I said...I suggest we say goodbye."

"OH, NO YOU DON'T—"

But the next second, Rae had turned invisible.

She watched their horrified reactions as she moved silently towards an open window, each one whirling desperately around as if hoping to catch her bumping into something so they could grab her then and there. Except she was too skilled for that. The Council hadn't labeled her a hazard to public safety for nothing. In her time since Kraigan had taken her first tatùs, she had accumulated more powers than anyone else on the planet. The limits of her ink where unmatched and unlimited. She was fairly sure she could slip away from four unarmed teenagers—

"Where the hell do you think you're going?"

An iron grip closed around her upper arm, and Rae shot back into focus with a gasp.

She always forgot that one of those unarmed teenagers was a psychic...

"Jules, you can't—"

A sharp crack shot across her cheek, followed by a rush of pain.

She fell back a step, clutching her face in shock. But it wasn't Julian who had slapped her.

It was Molly.

In all their years together, Rae had never seen her best friend so upset. People always underestimated Molly. Labelling her as a fashion nut, or a chatterbox, and generally looking the other way. Sometimes Molly would gleefully take advantage of this. Most of the time she simply didn't care. But looking at her now, watching as angry blue sparks shot out of her fingers and reflected in her eyes, Rae didn't think she had ever seen anything more terrifying.

"Rae Kerrigan," her low voice cut across the room, "I'm only going to say this once, so you listen up and you listen up good. If you *ever* try something like that again, if you *ever* try to sneak out in some brainless attempt to protect us..." Her eyes glowed ice blue. "I don't care how many powers you might have—so help me, I will walk right over there and kick your ass."

For a moment, Rae didn't care how many powers she might have either. She believed Molly with all her heart. Her face crumbled and she looked at her shoes. "I was just trying to—" A volt of electricity knocked her straight onto her back, and she pulled herself up with an obedient, "...okay."

For a second, no one seemed to know what to do.

Angel was looking at Molly for the first time with a bit of respect, and Julian was staring at Rae like he couldn't believe she got slapped. Only Luke looked unsurprised.

And, of course, there was Molly herself. "So, I'll ask again," she repeated calmly, straightening her jacket, "if you don't want to run, then what exactly do you suggest?"

Rae paused for a moment, thinking, before turning to Angel. "Is that still Gabriel?"

Angel glanced at the phone and nodded.

"Tell him we're going to Guilder."

"Guilder?" Luke exclaimed. "Rae—are you crazy?"

A ghost of a smile flitted across Rae's face. "We'll see."

"Kerrigan—*no!*" Julian took her firmly by the arms, looking deep into her eyes. "You expect us to let you walk straight into the lion's den?! What exactly are you hoping to find there?!"

Rae's heart was fluttering away in her chest like a deranged sort of butterfly, but for the first time all morning she felt remarkably steady.

"Proof."

They were to meet Gabriel in the middle of the park about halfway between Guilder and where they lived, close enough that they could see the fronts of both of their homes, but far enough away that they couldn't be seen by the PC guards. According to Julian, none of the Council guards were making any decisions for themselves. However, the five of them were, and that was enough for him to guarantee their safety.

There was a rustling in the trees behind them, and they spun around to see Gabriel sauntering towards them with his cocky smile.

"So, Kerrigan," he checked his watch, "by my estimation, it's been about a week since the last time you did anything reckless or crazy. Is it about that time?"

Julian shifted impatiently, but Rae offered him a small grin. "I got some good advice earlier, and I've decided to follow it. I'm going to get proof. And then tell Carter."

Gabriel's eyes twinkled as he nodded. "Good girl. In that case, I'm assuming you summoned me here for my shocking good looks and—"

"—and you're still one of the best fighters I've ever seen," she cut him off.

His whole face lit up with an adrenaline-fueled smile. "So there's going to be a fight, is there? Where exactly is this proof of yours...?"

Rae bit her lip. "In the Privy Council Headquarters at Guilder."

"Oh." For the first time, the smile faltered a bit. "So when you say there's going a *bit* of a fight, it's really going to be more of a slaughter—"

"Not as much as you might think," Julian inserted. "Mallins has ordered most all the PC guards to arrest Rae. We think they're on their way now. With any luck, by the time we get there the underground chambers between the Council buildings and Guilder will have just minimum security."

Gabriel met his eyes for a moment, before both men looked away. They knew firsthand the perils of even 'minimum security.' That same 'minimum security' had trained them. "Well, that's...great!" Gabriel shook it off with forced cheer. His eyes flicked around the nervous group of teens, before landing on Rae. "Lover boy isn't here amongst us?"

"No, he isn't," she said firmly. Then she raised her voice and repeated, "No, Devon isn't here," towards Julian, who looked like he had plenty to say on the matter.

She expected Gabriel to be smug—congratulatory, even. But he was none of those things. In fact, he was quite the opposite. "That's a bad idea." His smiling face had grown suddenly serious as he stared thoughtfully into her eyes. "He should be here, Rae, and I think you know it."

Her mouth dropped open in shock. "Why the hell are *you* of all people advocating for—"

"It's a bad idea," he repeated simply. "Devon can fight. He loves you, and he would fight for you. He should be here."

Behind him, Julian turned away and paced a couple of steps toward the trees. Rae's eyes followed after him, unsure as to where to look. But when she turned back to Gabriel to defend herself, he simply held up his hands.

"It's your call. Just know that while you might think it's what's best for him, it isn't. It's not what he would choose for himself." He left her with that and walked over to join Angel. Rae stared after him for a moment before darting a few steps after Julian, who was just slipping his phone back into his pocket.

"Julian Decker," she thundered, "you better not have just—"

"Relax." He shot her an icy glare. "It was just Carter. I told him where to go." His eyes drifted up to where Gabriel and Angel were talking by the trees. "Gabriel's right, though." He shook his head and muttered, "Like I ever thought I'd say that..."

"—they know who I am, Gabriel."

Rae's head snapped up, and she looked over to where the two makeshift siblings were having a hushed conversation. While Gabriel looked protective, Angel was equally as stubborn.

"And they would punish you for it," he hissed, placing an automatic hand on her arm. "But there's nothing wrong with who you are, Angel. It's nothing they can shame you for. It's nothing you have to apologize for."

Her lips turned up in a crooked smile. "But it's something I'll have to answer for."

"That's exactly what I'm saying," he insisted. "So why go? There's a villa in Tuscany with your name on it. We can meet you there when we're—"

But her sapphire eyes rested on Julian, still pacing back and forth between the trees. Her face softened to an exquisitely tender gaze, and when she looked back at her brother she simply shook her head.

He followed the movement with a hopeless sort of resignation, raking his fingers back through his hair with a sigh. "This is why I never fall in love. It makes you stupid."

Angel's eyes flashed to Rae before returning to him with a smirk. "Is that right?"

"Shut up." He stalked off. "I should have smothered you as a child…"

Across the grass, another hushed argument was being waged between Luke and Molly.

"It's not the same for you as it is for us," Molly insisted, standing up on her toes in a rather futile attempt to bring them to the same height.

"How is it not the same?" he fired back. "These people are my friends! I care about them. I want to help." He took her hands and lowered his voice softly. "I *love* you, Molly. I'm not just going to let you go in there alone—"

"This isn't your fight!" She stamped her foot as the garden suddenly went quiet. "This is our Council, our agency, our old school. Luke, I love you, too, but you work for the other side, and by now I'm sure all of them know it! If we were to get caught, I'm sure the repercussions will be severe. But if *you* were to be caught?

A Knight on Guilder soil?" She shook her head as all the blood drained from her face. "Luke, I have no idea what they would do to you..."

Molly was right. Rae acknowledged it at the same time that Angel caught her eye from across the grass. She gave a curt nod, which Angel returned before silently striding forward.

"I love you, Luke," Molly said again, with tears in her eyes. "I can't let you walk in there."

His eyes flashed, completely oblivious to what was going on behind him.

"I love you, too, babe, but unfortunately you can't stop me—"

His voice cut off suddenly as Angel rested a gentle hand on his shoulder. Every muscle in his body froze up at once, leaving him a beautiful statue in the morning sun.

"No, she can't," Angel murmured, giving him an apologetic grimace as she stepped back to survey her work, "but I can."

Molly rushed forward and jumped up again on her toes, pressing her lips against his frozen ones. "I'm so sorry, babe! I'm *so sorry*! But this will wear off in just a bit, and then I'll meet you when we're through. With any luck, we can still make that movie you wanted to see..." Her voice trailed off doubtfully at the look of fury darkening his eyes. "...or not..."

"Molls," Julian grabbed her by the wrist and started pulling her away, "we've got to go."

She flashed him one more look of goodbye, before joining the rest of them by the curb. "So how are we going to get there?" she asked glumly, glancing back at Luke. "The Council knows all of our cars. What if we pass them as we drive away?"

This time it was Angel who blushed, flashing Julian a quick look of apology before she lowered her eyes to the ground. "I...have a car we can take."

His eyebrows shot up in surprise. "When did you get a car? *How* did you ..." he hesitated nervously. "...how did you get money to buy a car? I thought all your finances were tied up with Cromfield."

"Now, Julian," she began rationally, "when you said 'what's mine is yours,' I took that to mean monetary compensation as well—"

"There's no time," Rae cut them off. "Deal with it later. We have to move." She shuddered, scared none of them were going to make it out alive this time. Her gut was telling her she should be worried—no, she should be terrified.

No one could fault Angel for style. That being said, as they raced down the freeway the five of them didn't exactly blend in.

"You got a Porsche." Julian closed his eyes and leaned his head back against the seat. The seat that he had unknowingly paid for.

Angel beamed back at him, completely unapologetic. "They call the color 'lipstick red.' It was the fastest one they had!"

He shook his head with a soft groan, but Gabriel patted him consolingly on the shoulder from the backseat. "You got off easy, man. On her seventh birthday, she stole my credit card and skipped off to town to buy herself a horse. When she couldn't decide which one, she ended up getting three."

"Which I had to return, if you recall," she defended herself, swerving around traffic.

He grinned. "What did you expect? That they would sleep in my room?"

"Well, actually—"

"There's the off-ramp!" Rae pointed, and Angel flew up the side toward the exit.

As their car rocketed down the country road, it struck her as suddenly strange that Angel wouldn't know that, because Angel had never come to their school. In fact, the closer they got to the sweeping grounds, the more Angel peered around with wide eyes.

It made Rae suddenly feel sorry for her. This should have been Angel's school, too. She should have known the off-ramp exit.

"Okay...where do I go?" she murmured, lowering her voice as they neared the parking lot.

Julian pointed to a side road up ahead. "Go there. It's a maintenance entrance. It'll be the last place to get checked."

The car slipped discreetly behind a dumpster—well, as discreetly as a fire-red Porsche could—and the five of them got out.

There wasn't a sound on campus. The school year wasn't set to begin for another few weeks, and for a few remaining days of summer Guilder was at peace.

Not for long... Rae thought as they walked silently up the grassy hill. It felt too quiet, making Rae uneasy. She'd never been at Guilder with it super quiet, or at least not unless it was the calm before the storm.

"Just remember," she cautioned in a low voice, "no matter what happens, we stay together. Jules is right: With any luck, there will only be one or two guards, and..."

All five of them froze in a line.

They had just reached the pathway that led to the Oratory, except they could hardly see the laneway.

They could hardly see it because every single agent who worked for the Privy Council was standing in their way. No one was heading to their houses, they were all waiting for them here.

The five of them were only given a second—a single second to acknowledge the trap.

Then the gates of hell opened and it was every man for himself.

With a chorus of screams and shouts ringing in her ears, Rae did the only thing she could think of. Bringing her hands together, she slipped into Camille's tatù and sent a wave of kinetic energy blasting across the lawn.

For a split second, it worked.

As the ground below their feet trembled and shook, the Council agents fell to the grass, giving her people enough time to dart through them towards the Oratory. But there were simply too many, and Rae looked on in horror as one by one, agents started to recoup. One by one her friends were going to fall. There was nothing she could do to stop it. She saw it unfolding before she had time to react again. Maybe it was Julian's tatù, maybe it was just reality.

She sure as hell wasn't going down with a fight, but she wasn't going to be able to save all of them—or any of them. She ducked as a large, burly look agent took a swing at her. She swung around and dropped down, kicked her foot out to take the giant down by his knees. He grimaced as his legs collapsed and he hit the pavement pretty hard. Rae spun around trying to see what was happening to her friends as she sent a shock into the guy. Not enough to kill him, but plenty to knock the guy out.

The first to go down was Angel. She was too far away for Rae to help.

Angel was firing a sea of tranquilizers into the crowd and freezing anyone who got to close. She had a damn good shot, but her ability was defensive and when a guy came up behind her and knocked the gun out of her hand, she didn't have time to react.

The man holding her was instantly frozen, as were the next five agents who tried to take her down. But it was the seventh agent who broke through and bashed her upside the head, sending her sprawling to the grass.

"ANGEL!"

Rae didn't know who shouted. Was it Gabriel or Julian? She was terrified, unsure if Angel could survive that kind of blunt-force trauma. It was a hard hit. Rae took down two agents as she watched Angel from where she stood.

Angel looked strangely peaceful—minus the trail of crimson leaking over her white hair—as if she'd simply fallen asleep. Then a heavyset man lifted her into the air and Rae could see her no longer. He was carrying her off somewhere.

They needed to prove to the Council what was going on. This was crazy. Rae charged forward with a guttural cry, flying towards the Oratory with everything she had. *The only way to stop this is to get the proof. The only way to save us all from a lifetime of incarceration is to break into that office.* Fight or flight. She sure as hell was going to fight.

She shifted her weight and kicked full force into the head of a woman who was running towards her who simultaneously grew spikes all over her body. The spikes disappeared the second the woman fell unconscious, but Rae barely had time to run before she heard another piercing scream.

A shudder ran through her whole body as she recognized who it belonged to. She froze another agent coming for her and then sent another two agents flying back to the trees with a gust of wind, she spun around just in time to see Molly's body crumple to the ground.

The ground around Molly was littered with the smoking bodies of a dozen or more agents. The woman who'd taken her down was kneeling behind Molly now, rolling up her sleeve as she gave Molly some sort of injection. Molly's body twitched suddenly as the drugs instantly hit home, and then went still. The woman picked Molly's limp body up and heading in the same direction the other agent had taken Angel.

Tears were pouring down Rae's face and it felt like she was moving in slow motion. It was just her, Gabriel, and Julian now. Against another fifty or so other agents that were still standing. *So help me, if you guys kill any of them, I'm going to unleash hell on you all.* Somehow she knew the PCs wanted them all alive, especially the hybrids.

USE MOM'S FIRE! USE IT NOW!

It was *all* Rae wanted to do. Her entire body ached for it. One wave of the blue flames, and everyone on the lawn would be simply swept away.

Except...it would also kill them.

And while she may be fighting to take down their very organization, *killing* them wasn't something she was willing to do. Unfortunately, that mentality was beginning to cause problems.

And not just for her.

She suddenly leapt backwards as the metal siding of a wall went flying past her. She looked around in shock to see Gabriel use it to knock down six or seven guards with a twitch of his fingers. But he tempered the force so as not to cause permanent damage, and a second later when they all got up again—charging towards him.

"Rae! Whatever you're going to do—*do it now*!" he shouted, bracing himself as they leapt upon him. He struggled against them, knocking one off before another managed to kick him. It didn't stop Gabriel, he'd been through a whole lot worse in his life than this. Pain wasn't something to slow him down.

"No!!" Rae couldn't believe this was happening. When had everything gone so wrong? Rae came upon another two guards; one apparently had the ability to flick his tongue out. He tried to wrap it around Rae's neck, only to find Rae freeze it with Angel's ability. It looked like it hurt a lot. "Dickhead," Rae hissed. Gabriel had cleared the way for her and she needed to take advantage of it.

Rae found the other guard, knocking him out a little too easily. She switched to Jennifer's tatù as she watched Julian.

With his uncharted ability to see the future, taking him down in a fight was virtually an impossible thing to do. The only problem was that in the chaos of the moment with a dozen bodies flying around, people didn't really make rational decisions. They tended to act on blind instinct.

With a strength Rae didn't know Julian had, he leapt up into the air, spinning around in a vicious kick that left three agents knocked senseless. He grabbed another by the throat, and was about to take down a fifth when Hank Montgomery, Guilder's head of security, jumped up behind him and grabbed him by the wrist.

Even across the lawn, Rae heard his arm snap. He was still doubled over when he was kneed in the face, and swept right back up into the waiting arms of the Privy Council.

A steady stream of blood poured down his face, and from the ashen color of his skin it looked like he was about to pass out. But right before he was blocked from sight, he looked up across the grass and saw Rae watching him.

For a frozen second, their eyes met. His lips moved and Rae was able to make out a single word. *Run.* Then someone shoved a bag over his head.

Without stopping to think, Rae sent a blast of electricity toward the guard she was fighting and then barreled over the people running towards her. She took off flying towards the Oratory again. Using Jennifer's leopard tatù to give her strength and speed, she sent anyone who touched her flying back into the trees. The bronzed double doors gleamed in the bright sun, finally there within reach. But the leopard didn't have the unparalleled senses of her fennec fox.

There was a sudden impact right behind her, and she whirled around in time to see Gabriel fall to the ground with a painful cry. Her eyes lifted up in horror, and fifty yards away she saw an ammunitions expert slowly lowering his gun to reload.

"Gabriel!" she shrieked, darting forward. A dark stain was slowly spreading across his shirt, blossoming out from his chest. "Don't move, I'm—"

But the second she reached him, he shoved her away, pointing behind her to the Oratory doors—just six or seven paces beyond.

"Rae," he gasped, trying to catch his breath, "you have to lock the doors behind you. The president's code—" he broke off with a sharp cry of pain, "—the code is *obiectis*. Carter told me. The others, they won't be able to get in." He gasped, swallowing as his face contorted with pain.

"No!" she cried, trying to help him once more. "I'm not leaving you here to—"

"It's not your choice," he said softly, hand trembling as he tried to stop the flow of blood. In true Gabriel fashion, he managed a small smile—even at the end. "Go."

Her eyes locked with his, memorizing his face before she turned on her heel. "Don't you freakin' die on me!"

"I won't," he whispered. "I'm much too pretty."

She grinned despite herself and finally tore away, still hearing his words because of Devon's tatù ability. A few seconds later, she reached the Oratory. No one was able to stop her as she raced, almost flying over them as she ran. She jumped up the steps and skidded to a stop in front of the familiar Oratory doors she'd gone through so many times.

"Shit! Shit! Shit!" She tried the password, spelling *obiectis* wrong as she tried the door. She redid it again, oddly wondering when they'd changed the code from just numbers to a keyboard. It didn't matter. She punched in the "s" of the passcode just as a final flood of agents poured towards her, obscuring Gabriel from view.

The sound of the door unlocking had her pulling at the door before it unclicked. She wrenched the heavy wood door open and slipped inside, pulling it tightly shut behind her and hitting the code on the inside wall with her free hand. The doors locked into place just as the first of the agents raced up the steps and banged on the door to get in. Rae sent a bolt of electricity at the code, killing it; sealing her in, and them out. This was either the most brilliant plan ever, or the stupidest.

After the deafening noise outside, it was suddenly whisper-quiet.

Rae turned around, her breath coming out in silent gasps as she hurried down the hall to the grand room of the Oratory. She glanced around the empty seats in the domed pavilion; it felt more like a funeral parlor than the room in which she had learned to use her tatù.

She shook her head, thinking about her friends who were risking everything outside to help her. She needed to help them. If one of them... She pushed the thought from her mind and ran across the room, the same room where she had fought Kraigan and nearly lost everything. She scoffed. She could really use his help right now. Running her hand along the familiar carved walls, she found the latch that would open a hidden door to take her into the bowels of the Privy Council chambers.

Angel, Molly, Julian, ... Gabriel. Images of them as they succumbed to the PC guards tore a sob from her throat. They'd all be physically hurt badly. What if the guards killed one of her friends?

She couldn't allow herself to think like that—or stop moving, otherwise all her emotions would catch up. She also couldn't think about her friends outside, or she would be overcome.

She had to keep her eyes on the target and keep moving.

Always moving.

She had a horrible feeling this was what the rest of her life was going to be like. Forever running away, always trying to prove herself. "I won't let that happen," she hissed to herself.

With the speed of the comic character, the Flash, she raced down the underground halls that led across the fields to the PC buildings. As she glided through the empty halls and corridors, down to Mallins' darkened office door, she couldn't shake the eerie feeling that she'd been this way before. That this was all following some sort of plan, somehow.

A plan not of her making.

She knew where Mallins' office was without needing to think about it. She straightened in front of his door and tried the doorknob. It was locked, but for the life of her Rae didn't have time. She stepped back, switched back into Jennifer's ink, and kicked it clear off its hinges.

It was a simple room. Not a lot of decorations or frills. Just a portrait of a stern-looking man mounted on the wall, and a plain desk sitting in the center.

Rae made a beeline for the desk, ripping open every drawer before she came to one that was locked. Then, with great relish, she ripped that one open as well.

...and stopped cold.

There were no files. There was no stack of evidence to exonerate her and her friends. There was nothing she could hold in her hand and use for their rescue.

There was just a computer connected to the desk that turned on when the drawer pulled open. A tiny computer with a blinking passcode.

"DAMN IT!" she screamed aloud, picking up the desk chair and throwing it to the corner of the room. It cracked and broke, all the pieces falling to the floor like wooden rain. She slumped down on the floor.

She would never get the passcode. Mallins would never give it up. The Council would never know the truth, and all of this—*all* of this—had been for nothing! They were all going to die... Trapped forever in a prison, never allowed to see each other again. Devon would never forgive her. What would her mother think? Maybe they would lie and say that they'd been killed or gone AWOL. The PC would probably blame Cromfield.

Her head fell back against the wall as a silent stream of tears ran down her face.

Well, sorry, Dad. Guess I'm not as invincible as you thought after all.

...Wait...

Her dad.

Her DAD!

Reaching into her pocket, Rae pulled out a tiny stone. The one she'd found along with the final piece of the brainwashing device beneath the Japanese maple. The same one she'd been carrying around ever since.

For the hundredth time, her fingers ran over the tiny inscription carved in the stone.

'*Vetitum*'

A familiar ink hummed suddenly in her skin... One that allowed her to understand all languages—courtesy of the future Queen of England.

Vetitum meant 'forbidden' in Latin.

Lifting her eyes slowly to the computer, Rae began to type. "Here goes nothing..." she whispered, then she hit 'Enter'.

A rush of warmth flooded through her chest, radiating through her entire body.

She stared at the screen, her eyes scanning the page, links, files faster than the human eye, courtesy of another tatù.

THIS WAS IT!

Everything she'd been looking for! Everything on the missing hybrids and the disaster that had befallen them! Everything that Mallins and the PC had tried so hard to hide!

The organization was called Vetitum as well—a secret hybrid genocide program perpetrated by select members of the Council and stretching back more than two hundred years.

Clever, Rae thought to herself as she ran her hands over the computer, *the organization and the password being the same word. No way to find it unless you already know what you're looking for.*

Well, not clever enough thanks to Simon Kerrigan!

With a look of triumph Rae pushed to her feet, pulling the computer from the drawer and cradling it under one arm, ready to break out and share it with rest of the world. Once she showed those who didn't know, they'd realize what was going on. It might take a bit of convincing, but she and her friends would be safe. Everything was going to be alright.

Then the light snapped on.

Victor Mallins stood in the doorway, looking at her with a cracked smile.

"What happened, Kerrigan? You found out the truth?"

Rae stopped dead in her tracks, clutching the computer tightly beneath her arm. Despite the fact that she'd found everything she needed to lock him away for the rest of his miserable life, Mallins didn't look the slightest bit afraid. He didn't even look worried about being trapped in a room with the infamous and 'potentially dangerous' Rae Kerrigan.

His smiled widened. It was awkward, like the man didn't really know how to smile properly. "I so hoped you would. It's why I dropped you hints about your house being bugged, to speed up your timetable. I even leaked false information to your friend at the Knights to make sure you would come straight here." He folded his hands together with satisfaction. "I have to say, Miss Kerrigan, you don't disappoint."

Rae shook her head, trying to clear it, trying to understand. "This whole time...you wanted this to happen? This was your end game?"

"No, dear girl," he chuckled. "I simply wanted you to go away. It's why I kept pairing you up with Mr. Wardell. I thought that either I could expose the two of you for having an illicit relationship, or at the very least you would be so disheartened that you would quit the Council and never come back. Well, no matter," he waved his hand and started walking slowly forward, "we're here now. Everything's going to end exactly the way it should. It always does."

Rae set the computer carefully on the floor behind her, watching his approach with cautious, uncertain eyes. What the hell was this old man doing? He was a telekinetic. A cool gift, to be sure, but not exactly a threat to her. "I don't want to hurt you..." she began slowly. Then her eyes flashed as she thought of everyone outside. "But you *are* going to pay for what you've done to my friends."

His dry laugh crackled through the room, setting her teeth on edge. "Oh, Miss Kerrigan, I've no intention of letting you hurt me. In fact," he reached out into a bookcase, pulling something out into the light, "quite the contrary."

The rest of the room seemed to fall away as Rae's eyes locked on his wrinkled hands.

A knife.

The exact same knife from her dream.

Moving slowly towards her.

In spite of herself, she took a step back.

This isn't possible. This isn't happening. Just use your powers, Rae—kick his ass!

With a look of determination, Rae slipped into the Gabriel's tatù and swept Mallins to the side with her hand.

Only...nothing happened.

Her breath caught in her throat, and she tried again—this time, using Haley's wind.

Nothing.

One by one, another power quickly rose to the surface, and failed her.

Levitation, flight, strength, even Molly's electricity. Nothing had any effect on the bastard.

She was standing with her back to the wall now, and he right in front of her, with that stupid grin.

"I don't understand..." she whispered, trembling from head to foot. "You're telekinetic—"

"No, Miss Kerrigan," he said softly, "That's only one of my powers. The other is a resistance to all forms of ink. An immunity to you and your horrible family tatùs. Simon's, Kraigan's, even your mother's."

Her eyes shot up in horror as the knife flashed in the air between them. It slid into her stomach, just as someone burst through the broken office door. Probably a guard to drag her to the prison dungeon. *Kinda looks like Devon.*

Millans grabbed her shoulder and jerked her forward, driving the knife in deeper. Her head sagged to the side and her eyes rolled as she tried to fight the pain. She swore she saw Devon by the door as her vision blurred with stars from the shock and pain radiating from her stomach.

"That's right, Rae," Mallins whispered as she slumped to the floor, "you're not the only hybrid in the Privy Council."

THE END
Last One Standing
Coming May 2016

DESCRIPTION

Last One Standing is the 11th Book of W.J. May's bestselling series, The Chronicles of Kerrigan.

Rae Kerrigan and her friends have finally crossed the line, and this time, there's no going back. After a violent standoff with the entire Privy Council, the gang wakes up under the protection of the last people they ever expected to see: the Xavier Knights.

Old bridges are burned. New alliances are formed. There's a storm brewing on the horizon, and unless they unite together—it will overtake them all. What they need, is time. But an unexpected visit from an old enemy sets off a spark, and suddenly, Rae's entire world is in flames.

Can she and her friends get the people they need together in time? Even if they can, will they ever be strong enough? More importantly, are she and Devon strong enough to survive what's about to come?

A dangerous game has begun and the only question that remains is: who will be the last one standing?

Sneak Peek

At the Rest of the Series Covers

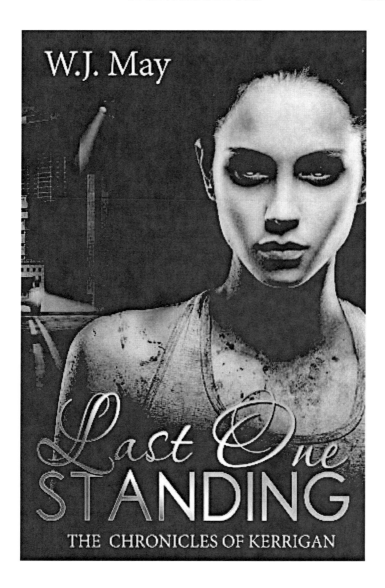

Note from Author

Thanks for reading (and hopefully enjoying Strength & Power). It's hard to believe that we are coming to the final stretch, the last 2 books of the series. I love writing about Rae's adventures, her friends and her life! I hope you guys don't mind sticking around for a few more rounds with Rae! And then learning what happened with Simon and Beth before Rae was born!

All the best, W.J. May

Newsletter: http://eepurl.com/97aYf

Website: http://www.wanitamay.yolasite.com

Facebook: https://www.facebook.com/pages/Author-WJ-May-FAN-PAGE/141170442608149

The Chronicles of Kerrigan

Book I - *Rae of Hope* is FREE!
Book Trailer:
http://www.youtube.com/watch?v=gHAwXxx8MU
Book II - *Dark Nebula*
Book Trailer:
http://www.youtube.com/watch?v=Ca24STi_bFM
Book III - *House of Cards*
Book IV - *Royal Tea*
Book V - *Under Fire*
Book VI - *End in Sight*
Book VII – *Hidden Darkness*
Book VIII – *Twisted Together*
Book IX – *Mark of Fate*
Book X – *Strength & Power*
Book XI – *Last One Standing*
Coming May 2016
Book XII – *Rae of Light*
Coming June 2016
PREQUEL – Christmas Before the Magic

CoK Prequel!

A Novella of the Chronicles of Kerrigan.
A prequel on how Simon Kerrigan met Beth!!
AVAILABLE NOW!

More books by W.J. May

Like most teenagers, Rouge is trying to figure out who she is and what she wants to be. With little knowledge about her past, she has questions but has never tried to find the answers. Everything changes when she befriends a strangely intoxicating family. Siblings Grace and Michael, appear to have secrets which seem connected to Rouge. Her hunch is confirmed when a horrible incident occurs at an outdoor party. Rouge may be the only one who can find the answer.

An ancient journal, a Sioghra necklace and a special mark force life-altering decisions for a girl who grew up unprepared to fight for her life or others.

All secrets have a cost and Rouge's determination to find the truth can only lead to trouble...or something even more sinister.

RADIUM HALOS - THE SENSELESS SERIES
Book 1 is FREE:

Book Blurb:

Everyone needs to be a hero at one point in their life.

The small town of Elliot Lake will never be the same again.

Caught in a sudden thunderstorm, Zoe, a high school senior from Elliot Lake, and five of her friends take shelter in an abandoned uranium mine. Over the next few days, Zoe's hearing sharpens drastically, beyond what any normal human being can detect. She tells her friends, only to learn that four others have an increased sense as well. Only Kieran, the new boy from Scotland, isn't affected.

Fashioning themselves into superheroes, the group tries to stop the strange occurrences happening in their little town. Muggings, break-ins, disappearances, and murder begin to hit too close to home. It leads the team to think someone knows about their secret - someone who wants them all dead.

An incredulous group of heroes. A traitor in the midst. Some dreams are written in blood.

Courage Runs Red
The Blood Red Series
Book 1 is FREE

What if courage was your only option?

When Kallie lands a college interview with the city's new hot-shot police officer, she has no idea everything in her life is about to change. The detective is young, handsome and seems to have an unnatural ability to stop the increasing local crime rate. Detective Liam's particular interest in Kallie sends her heart and head stumbling over each other.

When a raging blood feud between vampires spills into her home, Kallie gets caught in the middle. Torn between love and family loyalty she must find the courage to fight what she fears the most and possibly risk everything, even if it means dying for those she loves.

Daughter of Darkness
Victoria

Only Death Could Stop Her Now
The Daughters of Darkness is a series of female heroines who
may or may not know each other, but all have the same father,
Vlad Montour.
Victoria is a Hunter Vampire

Free Books:

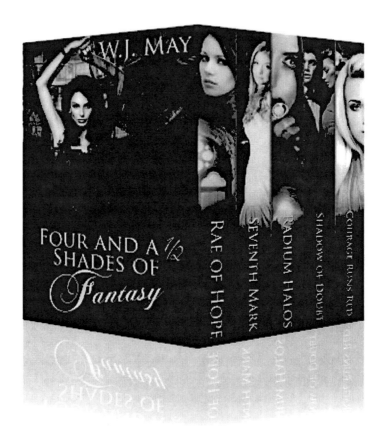

Four and a Half Shades of Fantasy

TUDOR COMPARISON:

Aumbry House—A recess to hold sacred vessels, often found in castle chapels.

Aumbry House was considered very special to hold the female students - their sacred vessels (especially Rae Kerrigan).

Joist House—A timber stretched from wall-to-wall to support floorboards.

Joist House was considered a building of support where the male students could support and help each other.

Oratory—A private chapel in a house.

Private education room in the school where the students were able to practice their gifting and improve their skills. Also used as a banquet - dance hall when needed.

Oriel—A projecting window in a wall; originally a form of porch, often of wood. The original bay windows of the Tudor period. Guilder College majority of windows were oriel.

Rae often felt her life was being watching through one of these windows. Hence the constant reference to them.

Refectory—A communal dining hall. Same termed used in Tudor times.

Scriptorium—A Medieval writing room in which scrolls were also housed.

Used for English classes and still store some of the older books from the Tudor reign (regarding tatùs).

Privy Council—Secret council and "arm of the government" similar to the CIA, etc... In Tudor times, the Privy Council was King Henry's board of advisors and helped run the country.

Don't miss out!

Click the button below and you can sign up to receive emails whenever W.J. May publishes a new book. There's no charge and no obligation.

http://books2read.com/r/B-A-SSF-QDUI

Connecting independent readers to independent writers.

Did you love *Strength & Power*? Then you should read *Seventh Mark - Part 1* by W.J. May!

Beautiful, quiet Rouge is trying to figure out who she is and what she wants to be. With little knowledge about her past, she has questions but has never tried to find the answers.

Everything changes when she befriends a strangely intoxicating family. Siblings Grace and Michael, appear to have secrets which seem connected to Rouge. Her hunch is confirmed when a horrible incident occurs at party. Rouge may be the only one who can find the answer.

An ancient journal, a Siorghra necklace and a special mark force life-altering decisions for a girl who grew up unprepared to fight for her life or others

.All secrets have a cost and Rouge's determination to find the truth can only lead to trouble...or something even more sinister.

Also by W.J. May

Bit-Lit Series
Lost Vampire
Cost of Blood
Price of Death

Blood Red Series
Courage Runs Red
The Night Watch
Marked by Courage
Forever Night

Daughters of Darkness: Victoria's Journey
Huntress
Coveted (A Vampire & Paranormal Romance)
Victoria

Hidden Secrets Saga
Seventh Mark - Part 1
Seventh Mark - Part 2
Marked By Destiny
Compelled
Fate's Intervention
Chosen Three

The Chronicles of Kerrigan
Rae of Hope
Dark Nebula
House of Cards
Royal Tea

Under Fire
End in Sight
Hidden Darkness
Twisted Together
Mark of Fate
Strength & Power

The Chronicles of Kerrigan Prequel
Christmas Before the Magic

The Hidden Secrets Saga
Seventh Mark (part 1 & 2)

The Senseless Series
Radium Halos
Radium Halos - Part 2
Nonsense

The X Files
Code X
Replica X

Standalone
Shadow of Doubt (Part 1 & 2)
Five Shades of Fantasy
Glow - A Young Adult Fantasy Sampler
Shadow of Doubt - Part 2
Four and a Half Shades of Fantasy
Full Moon
Dream Fighter
What Creeps in the Night
Forest of the Forbidden
HuNted
Arcane Forest: A Fantasy Anthology

Ancient Blood of the Vampire and Werewolf

CPSIA information can be obtained
at www.ICGtesting.com
Printed in the USA
LVOW10s1558311017

554455LV00011B/1072/P